GALWAY
GIRL

Also by Ken Bruen

KEN
BRUEN

GALWAY
GIRL

A Mysterious Press book
for Head of Zeus

First published in the UK in 2019 by Head of Zeus Ltd
This paperback edition first published in the UK in 2020 by Head of Zeus Ltd

9 7 5 3 1 2 4 6 8

A catalogue record for this book is available from
the British Library.

This book was set in 12-point Adobe Garamond Pro
by Alpha Design & Composition of Pittsfield, NH.

ISBN (PB): 9781838933081
ISBN (E): 9781838933098

Printed and bound in Great Britain by
CPI Group (UK) Ltd, Croydon CR0 4YY

Head of Zeus Ltd
First Floor East
5–8 Hardwick Street
London EC1R 4RG

WWW.HEADOFZEUS.COM

For

Caroline Diviney
"The Angel
of Bohermore"

and
Ban Garda Claire Burke
GG
Galway Girl and Galway Guard

with

Shuan (Siobhan) Quarter

and must mention

Eoghan McDonagh, Pat Cantwell, Danny Doherty

A Galway girl
Doesn't necessarily believe she
Is the best catch of all.
It's more that she'd love
You to prove
She isn't.

The first Guard was killed on a Friday.

The new Garda superintendent Mary Wilson (who was more than a little sick of the Supremes jokes) declared to the assembled Guards,

"This is horrendous."

Owen Daglish, a long-serving, not to mention long-suffering, sergeant, muttered,

"Not much escapes the bould Mary."

Sheridan, a loan to the beleaguered Galway station, gave him a look, said,

"Watch your mouth, Sonny."

Sonny!

Owen had a good ten years plus fifty pounds on the American.

American is used loosely as Sheridan gave the impression of being a Quantico guy but other elements, such as his fucked-up accent and Irish cynicism, pointed to a more likely Irish heritage but he was nevertheless, as he liked to cut it,

"A very influential *swinging dick*."

The Galway guys put it in their own tribal accent.

Like this:

"A prick."

Sheridan belonged to a new offshoot of Special Branch whose brief ranged wide and definitely included counterterrorism.

His pet obsession was Jack Taylor, the so-called PI who was on the *periphiery*, as he mauled the term, of so many recent violent deaths and yet stayed one beat ahead—or perhaps behind—an arrest.

It was a new young ban Garda named Nora McEntee who discovered the note at the murder scene. The forensic guys, horrified at the sheer violence of the scene, focused on the body and, owing to the pressure for rapid results, overlooked the most basic item.

The wastepaper basket.

Nora had been left to secure the scene as the professionals treated her like shite, with,

"Don't touch anything, girlie!"

You fucking believe it?

Girlie!

This was after she'd been told to grab some coffees for the teams, and the edict,

"Don't fuck up the pastries."

She sneered quietly at these macho blokes fussing over pastries.

How freaking gay were they?

Did they share the treats with her?

Or even refund the twenty euros for the designer java?

Did they fuck.

She'd picked up the trash basket out of curiosity and, lo and behold, a sheaf of parchment, curled at the edges. To age it? Or add grim authenticity?

Unfurled the paper and, smart girl, wearing crime scene gloves,
Read,

Unconsciously admiring the beautiful handwriting, in bold
Gothic script,

Ta bronach orm

When Wilson, the super, read this she was not pleased, especially as she had to ask the novice ban Garda, the aforementioned
Nora McEntee, to translate.

None of her close-knit team, the favored ones, spoke a word
of their native tongue. Time was, you didn't speak Irish or, worse,
didn't play hurling, you hadn't a Protestant prayer of joining
the Guards.

But now, as the writer Charlie Stella put it,

"Fugget about it!"

Best intoned in New York hard vowels.

Nora duly obliged, translated,

"I am sorry or, actually, I am heartbroken."

Snicker from one of the bright sparks with,

"Geez, really, which is it?"

Wilson, more than miles beyond patience, sent him to traffic
on the Headford road, the roundabout nightmare. He resigned.

Shortly after, thanks to his utter contempt for people, he
rapidly became a rising star in the charities racket.

Nora McEntee looked at the framed photos of Guards who
had died in the line of duty.

End of watch, as they say in the U.S.

She was gripped by the portrait of ban Garda Ni Iomaire.

Ridge.

She was Nora's hero.

Ridge had been noted for:

Being gay, in an obscenely misogynist force;

Her utter dedication;

Her fearlessness;

Her patience with new recruits.

Nora had gone to her a few times and she always said the same thing:

"Never back down and never, ever let the bastards see you are vulnerable."

She had also introduced her to

Kai tai yung.

A ferociously vicious form of self-defense that mutated in Galway from what had been a benign form of tai chi. To a Guard on the Galway streets when the clubs let out at four in the nasty morning and the fast-food joints were shutting their doors, gentleness was about as useful as a nun's rosary beads.

The blot on Ridge's almost brilliant career had been her relationship with Jack Taylor, a notorious drunk and former Guard. Despite repeated warnings, she had stayed in his corner even as her personal feelings toward him soured.

And soured fiercely.

Taylor had been MIA for many months after the death of his daughter.

Nora felt he was far from done. As Ridge had once said,

"Taylor always turns up, no matter how fucked he is, and God knows few do fucked like him, but he somehow drags all his bedraggled act in some form of together and shows up."

Ridge had gone silent for a bit, then added,

"There is something to be said for a man who does always show up. Not a lot, but you know something."

In those broken words Nora detected a kind of twisted admiration.

On any given
Day in Galway
You will hear at least one busker mutilate the
Words of "Galway Girl."
But, if you listen carefully,
Sincerity
Sometimes overcomes
The sheer banality
Of the performance.

Twyford

Makes the very best toilet bowls.

I know because I spent so much time lying on my back, under the bowl, having the first drink to be sick enough for the second one to stay down.

Hopefully.

It had been four months

Since my daughter had been shot dead

Right before my very eyes.

I missed Christmas.

In the sense it came and went and I lay under the bowl, if not the volcano. Then, mid-January, I began to cut back, no reason, maybe just sick of being sick.

Was even trying some exercises to restore some feeling to my shattered body.

If there are exercises for grief I don't know them.

I was living in an apartment off the Salthill promenade. I could look out across the bay, but now the once wonderful yearning I'd had was no more.

Years, years of that odd yearning, and I had never quite known for what it was I yearned. But now, no more mythical or mystical shite.

In a fit of blind rage and, yes, booze, I grabbed my favorite books, stumbled down to the beach, and began to fling them out across the ocean.

Pathetic?

You betcha.

A few days later, I was attempting to sip some coffee and not to smoke, least until the day grew up. A knock at the door. I shouted,

"Fuck off."

More banging.

Right.

I pulled the door near off its hinges, muttering,

"What."

A young female guard, ban Garda. And, oh Lord, she looked like a teenager.

Pretty, but something in the eyes, hint of granite.

She asked,

"Jack Taylor?"

I let out a frustrated breath, said,

"You're at my door, you obviously checked before you came, so unless you're a complete ejit take a wild guess."

She backed up, her body tensed, said,

"There is no need for that tone."

I turned, went back into the apartment, sat and stared at the ocean. She followed me in, with extreme care. She stood before me, said,

"I was a huge admirer of Sergeant Ridge."

I felt the guilt kick in, harsh, hard, and merciless, bit down, and said,

"How wonderful for you."

Threw her.

She had perhaps been schooled in how to deal with the likes of me but it wasn't working. I snapped,

"What do you want? You liked Ridge, so fucking what?"

She gazed around, seeking something to help. There was nothing, just my wall of hostility, but she did try, asked,

"There are no books?"

I laughed, said,

"You'll make a fine detective."

She held firm, said,

"You'll have heard of the recent death of a Guard."

I said nothing.

She did some figures in her head, trying to make a decision, then,

"The man was Ridge's uncle."

I was surprised. I tried,

"I'm sorry to hear that."

She glared at me and looked uncannily like Ridge. I asked, as I moved toward the door,

"Was there something else?"

She shook her head, asked,

"Is that it, you're sorry?"

I felt tired, opened the door, said,

"You need to go now."

She considered, then,

"They're right, what they say about you, that you're . . ."

She searched for some scotching term, settled on,

"Pathetic."

She was out in the hall. I shut the door as she was gearing up for more.

I thought,

"Nice wee girl."

Moved to the window, watched as she strode away from my apartment. A man got out of a car, crossed the street, walked right up to her, shot her in the face.

"We pursue all criminals
With vigor.
But if one of our own
Is murdered
We will pursue
With a ferocity
Of thundering devotion."
Superintendent Mary Wilson

Scott looked at himself in the mirror.

Saw:

Young man in his twenties,

Blond hair,

Scar along his left cheek, not blatant but noticeable,

Muscular build.

He said,

"No psycho vibe there."

He lived in a house off Taylor's Hill. His father, one of the first prominent Guards in the country, had bought it before the Celtic Tiger disaster.

Had said to Scott,

"When you join the Guards, you can live here, then just a smash 'n' grab to the station."

That was a vague attempt at humor. His father could be accused of many things and, indeed, in his long career, was accused of most, but humor, no.

He had serious plans for his retirement; death never occurred to him. He was washing his prized Audi when a thundering heart attack canceled his plans.

The funeral was a grand affair.

Lots of

Dignitaries,

Clergy,

Top brass.

Scott had to force himself not to puke when they handed the national flag to his mother after the burial. One of the numerous elite guys took Scott aside, whispered,

"Look, sorry you didn't make it onto the force."

Pause.

"But apply again. Maybe we can view you in a more favorable light."

Scott stood back, gave the man his practiced stare, the one he believed was ice. He asked,

"You think maybe if I work very hard, shite on everyone, perhaps one day I might be like you, a sad cunt?"

The obscenity shocked the man. He'd heard almost every epithet in his long career, but in a graveyard? He tried with,

"I'm going to cut you some slack seeing as the day it is."

Scott laughed, an eerie echoing sound among the headstones. He said,

"*Cut me some slack*? Dude, you are so far up your own arse you look like you couldn't cut air."

The man looked round for some of his troops. Nope, not a one; gone to the pub already. He decided to try the trusted older statesman gig, put his hand on Scott's shoulder, said,

"Son, you are troubled, I get that. Now go home and say your prayers."

Scott leaned back, made a gurgling throat sound as if he were drawing his very heart up, then spat full face on the man, said,

"Pray that."

Scott didn't immediately hit on killing Guards but the incident in the graveyard set the basis. In one of those weird moments of serendipity, he was stopped by a Guard ten minutes after leaving the cemetery, driving his father's Audi.

Was he speeding?

Yeah, okay, a bit.

He pulled over and the Guard ambled toward him, did the circular finger motion as seen on cop shows. Scott resolved to bite down, keep it together.

The Guard asked,

"License and insurance."

Fuck.

Scott tried,

"I'm coming from my dad's burial."

The Guard was chewing gum. Were they allowed that shit? Asked,

"Did I ask you where you'd been?"

Scott felt that resolve dip a little, said,

"See, it's my father's car and—"

The Guard cut him off with,

"Out."

Just that.

Designed to intimidate.

Scott began to open the door and the Guard slammed the door against him, then pulled Scott from the car, body-slammed him against the bonnet, muttered,

"Pup, think you own the world."

Then cuffed Scott, who said,

"Ah, for fuck's sake."

Scott was duly booked, appeared in court, got banned from driving.

He glared at the judge,

"I didn't do anything."

The judge threw in six months for what he called *impertinence*.

Scott was beyond outrage, screamed,

"You daft bollix, that's not impertinence, this is!"

Launched into a tirade of abuse.

Got an extra six months.

Plus a beating from a Guard when they took him down.

All in all, he served fourteen months.

Jail changed him utterly.

Word was out that he was the son of a Guard, so daily humiliations, hidings, abuse were his lot. Eventually, he toughened up, did the gym and worked on perfecting a nasty streak, learned the power of a psycho rep.

If asked by a new guy,

"What did you do?"
As in, why are you here?
He said simply,
"Guards."

On the day of his release the warden gave him what he liked
to think of as
The motivational speech.
A mix of self-help shite infused with smatterings of Dr. Phil,
Reader's Digest nuggets of wisdom, and his own distilled phi-
losophy of "no one is truly lost."
Scott stood before him, a sphinx of unknowing, waited.
The warden asked,
"So, young Scott, have you plans?"
Scott swallowed spittle, said deadpan,
"Yes, sir, a major plan of action."
The warden grinned, said,
"Splendid. Might I inquire further?"
Scott stared at him for a long moment, then,
"I am going to show the world my true worth."
The warden wavered, wondered if he was missing something,
suggested,
"Do tell."
Scott was tempted but he did need his release, so said,
"Service to the community."
Ah.

The warden gave him bus fare, an envelope containing enough to maybe pay for a burger, stood, said,

"I wish you the best of luck, young man."

Scott said,

"Luck has very little to do with it. It's all about determination."

Again, the warden wondered if there was a subtext.

Outside Scott breathed the air, said,

"Determined? Oh, yes, to kill as many Guards as counts."

For two years Scott *worked*, if such a term can be used, as an escort. A new flourishing biz for the new flourishing older lady.

Or, indeed, gentleman.

Scott had the looks and the careful cultivated air of an abandoned puppy.

His plan was to acquire sufficient funds, a safe base to launch his enterprise, all the while stoking his homicidal obsession.

The business he was engaged in eroded any traces of humanity that might still have lingered. If prison had fueled his rage, the escort trade added utter contempt to the mix.

The most valuable lesson he learned was to *charm in full sight*.

Scott rewrote the old truism on how to succeed.

Like this:

1. . . . . Steal freely
2. . . . . Kill randomly
3. . . . . Get with a Galway girl

He stared at those lines,

Smiled, said,

"See? Sense of humor."

Then the brain wave:

A Galway girl.

Wait for it—

"Who is a Guard!"

He had studied all the serial killer books, novels, and decided to leave a cryptic note after each kill, give a touch of mystique, and get the media hot.

Later, he'd abandon the notes he composed in Irish for the simple reason he got bored with it and, more important, he ran out of Irish; his education in his native tongue had been sporadic at best.

Aibhealai
Is the Irish word
For an exaggerator.
It's not much used as Irish people
Never exaggerate.

The shooting of Guard Nora McEntee caused a huge furor.

The city was on high alert, media screaming for the culprit to be apprehended.

He wasn't.

As the only witness, I was dragged to the station,

Not

. . . *to help with inquiries*

But more to be bullied, intimidated, shouted at.

Sheridan, the supposedly supercop, led the interview, demanded,

"Taylor, why are you always on the scene of shootings?"

I went with a vague truth, said,

"I have no idea."

He leaned right into my face, and I said, very quietly,

"Back the fuck off."

He was delighted, spun back, shouted to the Guards gathered,

"Hear that? He's threatening a Guard."

Owen Daglish, playing good Guard, said,

"Cut him some slack."

Sheridan fumed, snarled,

"Let's throw him in a cell, let him stew."

I said,

"Not a great time to be alienating the public."

Sheridan asked,

"What does that mean?"

The Garda commissioner was up to her arse in an alleged conspiracy to discredit a whistle-blower; the media were out for more dirt on the inner workings of the top brass.

Wilson, the super, breezed in, ordered,

"Cut him loose."

She looked at me, said,

"Try not to get in the way of the investigation."

I gave her my sweetest look, which is a blend of guile and deranged ferocity, said,

"Yes, ma'am."

The press were outside and Kernan Andrews of the *Galway Advertiser* shouted,

"In the middle of it again, Jack?"

I said,

"Buy me a pint and get an exclusive."

Kernan was too clued in for that old play.

I headed up Shop Street, gave a homeless guy a few euros, he asked,

"What will that do?"

"Ease my conscience."

Outside Garavan's, a young man, blond hair, dressed in black leather jacket, stared at me. He was not unlike a young David Soul and something in his attitude said he knew that. I asked,

"Help you?"

He gave a radiant smile, asked,
"Do you know the words of 'Galway Girl'?"

It was late when I got back to my apartment.
Something off.
All the mirrors had been smashed.
One sheet of paper, black with red letters, read

The walls of Jericho
Did
Not
Come
Tumbling down.

I asked aloud what you would.
I asked,
"The fuck is this?"

I went to the cemetery, wrapped in my Garda all-weather coat,
bitter, cold, vicious wind at my heels. There were so many graves
to visit and I muttered,
"I can't, I just can't."
But I could visit one.
New headstone, a frenzy of soft toys and wilting flowers all
around, the toys already soaked and beaten, here lay my daughter,
whom I barely had time to know before she was killed. I stood

there in wretched silence, unable to form words. I reached into my coat, took out the flask, chugged some Jay.

Didn't help but, then, nothing did.

I sensed being watched and turned to my right. A priest was standing about three rows from me, raised his hand in greeting, then approached me.

I have a terrible history with priests, full of lies, evasion, and downright betrayal.

He was young, mid-thirties, but his face already had that shocked expression of each day revealing the worst of humanity.

He held out his hand, said,

"I'm Father Paul."

I let it hang for a moment before I took it, said,

"Jack. Jack Taylor."

He looked at the grave, asked,

"Would you like me to give a blessing?"

My mood turned nasty, well, nastier. I asked,

"How much will that cost?"

Shoot
   the
      Woman
         First.
            Wallace Stroby

Jericho revisited her grand plan of chaos:
Recruit two dumb men; fuck 'em over in every sense,
Then kill two women.
She said aloud,
"The twos rule,"
As she fingered the two G's on a chain around her neck.

Prison for Scott was punctuated by:

Beatings,

Assaults,

Slow gym building,

Until he was celled with a hacker.

They jelled and Scott learned the basics of the hacker's art.

Freed, as he prepared his Guard blitzkrieg, he had the bright idea of getting a female Guard as a girlfriend. This in mind, he hacked the Garda personnel file.

Nora McEntee caught his eye. He muttered,

"You'll do nicely."

Stalked her slowly, then approached her in the pub one night, asked,

"May I buy you a drink?"

She gave him the measured Irish woman scan, deadly in its scrutiny, and he was found wanting. She said,

"No, don't think so."

Her friends tittered.

Tittered!

At him?

She was no fucking prize, he thought, and for a good-looking dude like him to throw her a crumb?

The fuck was with that?

Two days later Scott killed his first Guard.

Noel Flaherty, a close friend of his father, was, as Scott muttered,

"A prize bollix."

He was, by sheer coincidence, an uncle of the late Garda Ridge.

Scott had found his father's Colt .45, the authentic Old West gig, a present from law enforcement in Arizona. He had attended a conference there and made friends with the top cops.

This weapon was lovingly cleaned, oiled, and locked away again every week. Only once had Scott been allowed to hold it.

His father had said,

"If you man up, maybe someday you might be allowed to actually load it."

Right.

A box of six bullets.

So, six Guards.

Why not?

Noel Flaherty lived in one of the old fishing cottages in Clad-dagh, alone since his wife died. Scott easily broke in through a piss-poor lock on the back door.

Cops were notoriously lax at home protection, thinking,

"Who'd have the balls to burgle us?"

Flaherty was watching a video of the Galway hurling team win the All Ireland, roaring and cheering as if he were at Croke Park.

Scott stepped in front of the TV screen, said,

"The match has been canceled."

Scott was dressed in ski mask, black jeans, hoodie, his whole body alight. He slipped out the back door, left a note to give the dumb cops something to puzzle over.

The actual note meant nothing to him but he thought it added a nice air of intent.

Outside, he was coming from the back alley and not only was the damn mask itching but the fooker was hot. Sweat rolling downs his face, he whipped it off, gulping large bolts of oxygen.

Realized the gun was still in his hand.

Fuck.

Careless.

Then noticed a girl leaning against the far wall, smoking a cig, dressed like a Goth punk. He raised the gun, thought,

"Shite, only five bullets left."

The girl pushed away from the wall, gave a malicious smile, said,

"Gotcha."

On her second line of coke, Jericho said aloud,
"First dumb fuck selected."

How to succeed
In Galway
Without really trying:
1. Play hurling.
2. Feed the swans.
3. Get with a Galway girl.

I was coming out of McCambridge's, having bought a six-pack of Lone Star, the longneck brand. Rachel, lovely girl who works there, asked me,

"Is that a good beer?"

What to say? I said,

"Makes me long to go to Texas."

Which was kind of true.

Outside, I paused, lit a Marlboro Red, hitting all the U.S. notes. A guy passing said,

"Where's your ash?"

Threw me. WTF, did he mean on the cig?

He indicated his forehead, which had a gray smudge. The penny dropped.

Ash Wednesday.

Where does the time go when you're in fucking bits?

I wanted to stay in U.S. mode, snarl the American term for sex.

"Getting your ashes hauled."

Or maybe some literary quip on T. S. Eliot, but I couldn't be bothered, said,

"Forgot."

He eyed me, then,

"Let's hope the Lord doesn't forget you."

Sweet Jesus.

A Holy Roller.

I snarled,

"God forgot me somewhere in the middle of the Celtic Tiger."

I went to Freeney's, truly your old-style Galway pub, no frills, no hen parties, no newly rich on paper gobshite with the narrow suits, skinny ties, and those crocodile brown, long shoes that were, as O. J. Simpson had once termed his own footwear,

"God-ugly suckers."

If you have to quote Simpson in any context you are fucked beyond any reckoning. Freeney's even have fishing tackle on display in the window and hooch in earthen jars. I see that, I long for a childhood in bygone Ireland that I think really existed only in the pages of Walter Macken.

How do you live when your child was murdered?

You try to read the papers, the headlines engorged with the furious debate raging on . . . *Repeal the Eighth Amendment*.

You had:

Pro life,

Pro choice,

The Church,

Fundamentalists,

And bitterness fueled with ferocity that had opposing placards

Like this:

Baby killers

Who owns women's bodies?

The world had somehow survived the first year of Trump,

If barely.

At the Winter Olympics, saw the incredible:

A handshake between North and South Korea.

Phew-oh.

I initially tried to struggle through my grief by immersion in darkness, read the books of ferocity:

Chris Carter

Herbert Lieberman's *City of the Dead*

Joseph Koenig

Derek Raymond's Factory novels

Drew the line at actually watching the *Saw* franchise but I was that close to out-and-out weirdness.

A student wandered in looking lost, wearing a Donegal GAA jersey and a dazed expression. The bar guy, great ole Galway trouper named Mac, intercepted him, barked,

"Park it elsewhere, son."

A relatively new trend in the city:

Donegal Tuesdays.

The students, dressed in the counties' T-shirts and jerseys, drank like lunatics and generally terrorized the town. Oh, and despite the freezing February weather, they wore no coats.

I was told,

"*It's so uncool to wear coats!*"

Not to mention fucking idiotic.

By all that is wonderful in insane Irish logic, this week of Donegal Tuesdays coincided with the Annual Novena in the cathedral.

Church bells intoned three times daily and hawkers from every nonreligious pocket of the land set up stalls selling

Padre Pio relics,

Scapulars blessed by various popes,

Medals to ward off all save misery,

And enough bottles of holy water to stop a zombie apocalypse.

Drunken students, cowed pilgrims, lashing rain . . . what's not to love?

A young man stared at me from the counter, dressed in a fine suit, had the look of a furtive apprentice accountant. I snapped,

"The fook you looking at?"

The bar guy gave me the look that said,

"Chill."

The man slipped off the stool, sauntered over, gave me an appraisal not unlike an undertaker, as in,

"How big need the coffin be?"

He asked in a Brit accent,

"You Jack Taylor?"

I nodded.

He sat, took a long draft of his pint of cider, said,

"You were a friend of my dad's."

Jeez, that covers a multitude and very little of it good. I stalled, tried,

"And he is/was?"

The name he gave shattered me.

Years before, this name had been my best mate until . . .

Until . . .

I drowned him.

The name he uttered:

"Stapleton."

I don't do friends well.

It starts out okay but they soon tire of the drinking and my temper.

Stapleton seemed the exception.

As the Americans say, "He had my back."

Until I realized he was slowly but surely planting a knife there.

We'd ended up on Nemo's Pier, the scene of so many of my worst moments.

In the midst of a ferocious storm.

Not quite as fierce as the storm in my heart.

I threw him into the water, knowing he couldn't swim, and despite the wind I thought I heard him scream.

My own scream was,

"Fuck you."

The only difference between
A grave
And a rut
Is the dimension.

I was still reeling from the revelation of Stapleton's son. Stapleton had been one of the best friends I'd ever had.

But

I ignored the old chestnut

. . . *keep your enemies closer.*

He was a force of malignant nature. His past included:

Paramilitary time,

British army,

Sundry mercenary black ops.

Or so it was rumored.

In Galway, he'd reincarnated himself as an artist.

If you want to pose as an artist,

Wannabe poet,

Author,

Galway is your nirvana.

All you have to do is declare yourself so,

Carry a copy of Joyce/Beckett/Heaney—

The more battered the copy, the more convincing—

And, best of all, you never have to read the fuckin' things, just go "*Ah,*"

Shake your head a lot,

Take deep breaths before answering a question,

And, most vital,

Scratch yourself

A lot.

Oh, a combat jacket and scuffed Docs add to the portrait.

And be on the dole as you avail yourself of all the arts council grants.

Attend the lit parties.

Network like a frenzied banshee.

Stapleton fooled me for a long time, I truly believed he was my mate.

Phew-oh.

Turned out to be one of the most cunning ice psychos I'd ever had the bad karma to meet. When I drowned him, I said with utter conviction,

"Good fuckin' riddance."

Meant it then, mean it now.

I stood outside Freeney's, lost in the past. A guy passing said,

"Hey, Taylor, have you been to the new pub in Bohermore called Harry's, like some Hemingway vibe, you think?"

All this dark remembrance needed some serious drink, so I went into Harry's off Water Lane, a new *boutique pub.*

Yeah, God help us.

Translate as,

"Locals not welcome and we have fierce notions."

In I went, ordered a hot one. The bar guy had a ponytail—clue one to hostility.

He asked in a beat above disdain,

"What will Sir have?"

Sir.

In fuckin' Bohermore?

Seriously.

I said, in a measured tone,

"Large hot one, Guinness chaser."

Pause.

Then,

"Will Sir require cloves?"

Fuck.

I snapped,

"If Sir requires cloves, Sir will be quick to mention it."

Then dialing it back, I tried,

"Bitter out there."

He near sneered.

"It *is* February."

Gotcha.

I said,

"I didn't know a reprimand was part of the service."

Took my drinks, moved to a window, and no sooner than that,

A woman passing did a double take, came in.

Uh-oh.

She had been a showstopper in her day, maybe fifty now but a kind of classical beauty lingered as testament to her former glory. Grief or its neighbor had played hard with her features.

She asked,

"Mr. Taylor?"

"No,"

I said.

"But I am often mistaken for that reprobate."

She asked,

"May I sit?"

Wouldn't you fucking know it, the surly bar guy then decides to be affable, goes,

"Need a refill?"

'Course, he could just have been mind-fuckin'.

The woman said, "You are Mr. Taylor."

I looked at the woman, smiled, said,

"Busted."

She allowed a minute smile but fleeting, said,

"I know it's rude to bother people when they're having some quiet time."

"'Tis,"

I said.

"Rude."

She wrung her hands, a gesture that pains my very heart, despair writ small. I noticed her nails were bitten to the inflamed quick, so fuck it, I asked,

"What's the story?"

Thinking, Oasis, "Morning Glory."

She began,

"My name is Amy Fadden. My daughter, Rachel, is ten."

Sob.

"Was ten.

She was drowned, deliberately."

Phew.

I asked,

"Who drowned her?"

Long silence.

Then,

"A boy named Jimmy Tern."

She looked at me in utter horror, said,

"Jimmy Tern is eleven."

"Tern?"

I echoed.

She nodded, said,

"The mayor's son."

Oh, fuck.

I asked, with skepticism leaking all over my tone,

"He *drowned* your daughter?"

She said that Tern, Rachel, and a girl named Alison were fooling around in a boat on the canal. Rachel fell in and then Tern leaned over the side of the boat and held Rachel's head below the water until . . . until . . .

God in heaven.

I tried,

"Go to the Guards, get what's-her-name, Alison? To tell them what occurred."

"She won't."

I shook my head, asked,

"What on earth can I do?"

She raked her nails along the table, a screeching sound, said,

"Make him talk."

I felt for her. God knows I knew the grief of losing a child, and I also knew the price you pay for cold and ruthless revenge. I had taken such a step and, as hell is my dark witness, I was glad and am still glad I killed the fucker who took my child. But would she be able to carry the burden of revenge and, worse, or rather more to the point, would I be able to carry the extra weight of payback on her behalf?

She had said,

"Make him talk."

But we both knew she wanted the ice-cold rush of retaliation. I stood up, said,

"I will talk to him. That I can do, but anything else and I can't promise what will ensue."

She grasped my hand, kissed it, swore,

"I'll make you glad you did."

I left her with a pounding in my blood, my heart hammering, and my hand scorched from where she'd kissed it.

"I think that crime writing is quite serious
And has been accepted as such, but it is about crime.
I couldn't write a poem about kiddy pornography.
Perhaps my vocabulary is closer to the gutter than not
But it doesn't mean I'm not serious about what I'm writing."

Andrew Vachss

I was a little over the limit, truth to tell, and asked my own self,

"Who gives a fuck?"

Looked out across Galway Bay, all the way to the desired U.S., and the ocean rolled back a resounding

"Nobody."

One of the few lights in my befuddled life was living in an apartment that was opposite the bay. I never ceased to stare and yearn.

I got home after a few fumbled drunken attempts with my key, and was immediately alert.

Somebody had been in again.

My nine-mm was hung in a pea jacket near the door. I slipped it out and ratcheted a round, then, holding it two-fisted like the movie guys, I entered the living room.

What I saw spooked me fast and hard.

In the center of the coffee table a gleaming crystal skull.

I scanned the room. Moonlight cast its beam and gave an eerie glow to the skull. I let the nine rest in one hand, headed for the drinks table, uncorked a bottle of Laphroaig, a present from Johnny Depp.

Kidding.

I got it from the manager of McCambridge's at Christmas.

It takes a practiced dipso to get the cap off, splash a shot or two into the tumbler, knock it back. It's a finely tuned act with one hand and even more impressive without taking my eyes off the skull.

Fortified, I approached the table and, fuck me, was I seeing things?

Embedded in the center of the skull was an insignia—

Of the Garda Síochána.

Scott had inherited his father's house, a rambling mess of overgrown garden, built from old Galway granite, and it had an Edgar Allan Poe vibe.

Suited Scott to a maniac T.

His mother, Valiumed to the hilt, asked.

"Is it okay if I stay in the west wing?"

Scott laughed, a malicious, glee-free sound. He said,

"*West wing!* How very fucking Anglo-Irish."

His mother tut-tutted, scolded,

"Language."

Scott glared at her. She didn't have her husband to back her passive-aggressive taunts. He moved right in her face, asked,

"How polite is this? Get the fuck out of the house by close of business, meaning this evening."

A mournful dirge she began was interrupted by a special delivery package

Addressed to:

Scott,

Son of prominent dead Garda,

Taylor's Hill,
Galway.
The courier remarked,
"Odd form of address."
And lingered on the doorstep
For a tip/explanation?
Scott hit his head in mock exaggeration, said,
"Oh, silly me, you're waiting for a tip."
The courier gave an attempt at a modest grin. Scott said,
"Here's a tip: mind your own fucking business."
Scott bounced the package in his hand, puzzled.
Opened it carefully.
A disc fell out with *play me* inscribed.
He did.
A shaky video that showed him crossing the street, shooting Nora McEntee, then hurrying away. The camera panned to reveal a man in a top-floor apartment with a shocked expression. There was a short music track to accompany the shooting.
"Galway Girl."
By Steve Earle.
Scott then noticed a sheet of paper, read,

Scotty,
    Yah mad bastard.
    The face in the window is an ex-cop, Jack Taylor.

You need to exercise due care.

You my bitch now.

xxxxxx

Jericho

February 2018

The Beast from the East.

Brutal storms, blizzards, snow coming from eastern Europe

Nigh paralyze Europe.

Ireland goes into panic mode.

Three days of utter chaos as the shops empty of food

And a sense of Armageddon prevails.

Sales of toboggans are staggering.

Who knew we even knew what a toboggan was?

Most things we can make an effort at,

But snow?

We don't do snow.

Ireland stayed in lockdown for five days.

Heavy snow altered the city landscape in a sort of beautiful, flawed fashion.

Supermarkets ran out of all supplies and for two days there was an actual curfew because of the velocity of the winds.

Horror of all, even the pubs shut.

Grim days.

TV news rolled out weather experts who doled out increasingly dour doom-ridden forecasts. I holed up in my apartment, watching the ocean at its fiercest, at its finest.

Had to ration my booze lest the storm continued longer.

Eerie to see the streets so deserted.

On the Saturday, knock on my door, opened it to a young man. Took me a moment to recognize him.

Stapleton's son.

Fuck.

I asked,

"How did you know where I live?"

He gave an odd smile, asked,

"May I come in? I brought supplies."

He did indeed have many bags, bulging with food, booze, so I let him in.

Asked,

"How'd you get all this when the town is literally shut?"

He said,

"My job."

"Yeah, what do you do?"

"I burgle."

Not many sane replies to this, so I went with,

"Oh."

He grabbed a bottle from one of the many bags, said,

"Let's brew up some hot ones."

I held up my hand, said,

"Whoa, I don't even know your name."

He looked at me, went with,

"The fuck does that matter?"

Said,

"Terry. Mundane, eh?"

I took the bottle from him, shoved it back into the bag, said,

"Okay, Terry, thanks for the thought."

I gathered up the bags, pushed them at him, opened the door, said,

"You take care now."

His face turned in an instant, the laid-back guy gone and now a hard stone chill. He said,

"You fucking owe me, Taylor."

I nearly laughed, said,

"Don't think so, pal, now on your way."

"You murdered my old man."

I near stammered,

"That is ridiculous."

He smirked, said,

"Not according to the people I talked to."

I tried to stay cool, asked,

"Any of them offer proof, evidence, even motive?"

He weighed his words, then,

"Apparently you believed he was responsible for the death of a friend of yours."

I shook my head, said,

"This is Galway. What they don't know, they invent. Go live your life, leave the past be."

He gave me a long look, said,

"Keep looking over your shoulder, Taylor, I'll be around."

I shut the door in his face.

Did I consider him a threat?

These days, just about everything seemed threatening. He was just one more dark line in a story embedded in darkness.

"If his view of life would scare the bejesus out of you,
Nevertheless, he had the courage of his convictions,
And that's more than the rest of them had."

George V. Higgins on G. Gordon Liddy,
Watergate burglar

I thought a lot about Amy Fadden and the alleged murder of her daughter.

If, and major *if*, she had been drowned by the mayor's son, then a full-scale clusterfuck was in the cards.

Mayor Sean Tern, not a popular guy and very much of the old school type of politics, the

Nod and wink,
Slap your back,
Don't tell and never show gig.

But he had the juice, meaning money and friends of influence.

What the hell, I felt in the mood for a scrap.

Dressed in white shirt, loose tie, my Garda coat, 501s, Doc Martens. Very much a mixed metaphor, a blend of tough and yet *one of the guys*.

Headed for town, checking over my shoulder for Stapleton's son. No doubt he was off preparing a new burglary.

The ferocious beast of a storm had ended after a week of dire conditions and now came the burst pipes, power cuts, and the government assuring us that we'd be back in business soon.

Really.

The receptionist at City Hall was ice in clipped speech.

Like this,

"His lordship doesn't see walk-ins."

Fine.

I asked,

"He's a lord now?"

Didn't merit her reply, so I said,

"It's regarding an allegation about his son."

Still no move, so I pushed.

"Guess it's the newspapers, then."

Immediate reaction and a hurried,

"Wait here."

She fucked off down a long corridor, all bristling anger.

Five minutes and she returned with a thin guy, wispy hair, tight suit, tighter face, and an air of

"I deal with assholes, fast."

I said,

"You're not the mayor."

He allowed a thin smile to leak sideways from his curled lip. He was going to enjoy this.

Or so he thought.

He said in a withering tone,

"I deal with the more trivial of the mayor's businesses."

I asked,

"They allow you a name?"

He sighed, said,

"Mr. Cahill."

I said,

"You have lovely manners."

He made a show of checking his watch, important business waiting, demanded,

"Who are you?"

I held out my hand, which I knew he'd ignore, said,

"Jack Taylor."

A dim light ran across his eyes, then,

"Oh, Lord, yes. Some kind of raggedy-arsed private eye."

I said,

"A serious allegation has been made against the mayor's son."

He chuckled, made a face of deep annoyance, said,

"The alleged accuser has withdrawn her ridiculous charge."

Fuck.

I waited.

He turned on his heel, not even a word of dismissal. I shouted,

"God bless."

I found Jimmy Tern at the canal, the last place you'd think he'd be.

Accused of drowning a girl, why would he return there of all places?

I knew him from Instagram. He was all over social media, and if his posts were any indication he was a cocky little bollix.

Tall for his age, dark hair in what was once a Beatle cut, dressed in an expensive navy tracksuit, and the latest trainers—the ones that went for upwards of 250 euros.

How would I know that?

Mainly from utter astonishment for what we in our naïveté still called sand shoes.

Jimmy was obviously leader of the pack, and a motley bunch they were: two boys who were the followers and three girls drawn to the bad boy vibe.

Jimmy was in his element, uttering directives to the gang.

He spotted me and a vague hostile bravado drew him near. He demanded,

"Wotcha want, pedo?"

I liked him already.

I said,

"I'm here to make you famous."

The new irresistible lure for the young.

Fame.

Didn't matter how and talent wasn't even in the neighborhood, just be a YouTube viral star.

He moved closer, asked,

"How?"

No question as to why.

Just get me there, fast.

I said,

"Child killers are hot now."

Rocked the little bastard.

He faltered for a moment, looked to his gang who, as one, were staring at their feet, then,

"Fuck you, my dad will have you for slander."

I said,

"But then we'll get you to a court and, who knows, a lot can happen there. Least the world will see your face."

He spat at me.

I said,

"You really are a nasty little prick, aren't you?"

Truth to tell, I wanted to wallop him, a lot, went with,

"Can you swim?"

The gang were slowly slithering away. He snarled,

"Of course I can swim, you moron."

I made a fast move toward him and he backed away, lost his balance, into the water. One of the girls laughed. He struggled for a moment then swam to the bank. I said,

"Nice stroke but you need to work on your dive."

"Then
I had the kind of dreams
Where big black birds try to
Pluck your eyes out
And you wake up
With the sheet knotted around you
Like a vine."

Mercedes Lambert, *Dogtown*

The fine Australian crime writer Peter Temple died aged seventy-one.

Ireland beat Scotland to win the Six Nations, and if they beat England at the dreaded Twickenham they'd have the Grand Slam.

We hoped, as this fixture was set for St. Patrick's Day, we had some hard-core charm on our side.

I Never Sang for My Father,

A grueling emotional ride with Gene Hackman, was on cable.

Did I watch it again?

No.

My own father was great.

Few people in my life had such an impact on me. He was that rarity, a good decent man, as opposed to my mother, the walking bitch.

He once said to me,

"I'm not an aggressive person and I rarely feel aggressive but sometimes . . ."

Pause.

"I do feel the need to cut loose, be reckless, and be a man."

I was twelve and this meant little to me. I always felt aggressive and vented on the hurling pitch.

My father worked on the railways. After a particular shift, his overtime and a win on the horses collided to leave him with the grand total of 1,500 pounds.

A friggin fortune in those days.

He hadn't yet told my mother and I think he was on the verge of handing it to her when she from nowhere exploded,

"When do I get a new kitchen set?"

Before he could flash the money, she sneered,

"What kind of pathetic excuse of a man are you? I could have married somebody in the Post Office."

He grabbed his coat, said,

"C'mon, Jack."

And we were out of there.

Walked to Salthill, my father silent most of the way.

I didn't care. As long as I was in his company, my world had a foundation.

The Castle Inn had just opened and was doing a thriving business, mainly due to the extras from *Alfred the Great* filming in Galway then.

They were earning mad money as Anglo-Saxons fighting draftees from the Irish army.

For a pound, you'd get eight pints, ten cigs, and change for chips on the way home.

My father ordered a pint and a Paddy chaser.

Boilermaker.

We didn't know such terms then, it was simply a short one to keep the pint company. He got a *mineral for the boy*.

All soft drinks, which were either Claddagh orange or bitter lemon, came under the heading of that.

My father rarely drank spirits, had said,

"Road to hell."

True that.

The very first Wimpy bar was due to open and we'd soon be able to try the very first hamburgers to hit the country.

My father drank fast; again, unusual for him, said,

"There's a poem titled 'If.'"

He paused.

Then,

"Lines in it that if you can make a pile of your winnings and roll them on one turn of the dice, it says . . ."

He looked at me,

"You'll be a man."

This seemed to deeply sadden him.

We crossed to Claude Toft's, the only casino in the town. Such things as online betting, a myriad of bookies were all in an unimaginable future.

My father went straight to the roulette table, took the money out of his jacket, looked at me, the wad of cash in his right hand, hovering, asked,

"Red or black, Jack?"

I near whispered,

"All of it?"

He nodded.

I watched the wheel spin, looked up into my father's face. He said,

"Choose."

"Upon my return to Ireland,
I told my friends about *Irish people*
Who had *done well.*
Not everybody was happy for them.
Fuckers
Thieves
Probably born with it."
  Darach Ó Seaghdha, *Motherfocloir*

When I was a child, the sternest warning uttered by parents went,

"*Don't ever bring Guards to the door.*"

Now, the day before St. Patrick's Day,

The Guards came to my door.

Loud, hard, and shouting.

Slammed me up against the wall, screaming,

"Don't fucking move."

As if.

I wanted to say,

"I paid my TV license."

But levity was not in the air.

At the Guards station, I was flung into an interview room, left to wait.

Time droned on until supercop himself, Sheridan, appeared.

He was supposedly on loan from the States but his accent danced a wobbling reel between broad New Jersey and Shantalla.

He was dressed in FBI mode: tight clean-line suit, tiny mic in the ear, buzz-cut hair. He turned the chair around so he sat cowboy style, arms resting on the back. He had watched way too many movies. He began,

"You're like seriously fucked, Jack."

I waited a beat, then,

"What else is new?"

Amused him.

Slightly.

He said,

"No wisecracking your way out this time, buddy."

Buddy?

I said,

"You're not my buddy."

He reached into his jacket, produced a cigarette, lit it, blew an impressive cloud of smoke, looked at me, waiting for a comment.

He got none.

He asked,

"You know a young boy named Jimmy Tern?"

Uh-oh.

I said,

"A spoiled brat."

He blew more smoke, then,

"His friends say you threw him in the canal."

For fuck's sake.

I said,

"For fuck's sake."

He got right in my face, asked,

"Why'd you kill him?"

God almighty.

I said,

"He's dead?"

Sheridan said,

"As a doornail."

* * *

Some beliefs just defy logic, and no matter how much you rebel
against it the notion persists.

Like this:

If you need a lawyer, our genetic code, our history, kicks in
and we want a guy with three essentials:

Brit accent

Anglo-Irish roots

Disdain

And, not essential but valued,

Double-barreled name.

I got

Jeremy Brett-Shaw.

That hyphen is worth the exorbitant fees.

But

He didn't get to me until I'd been locked up two days,

Missing a wedge of real sporting history.

On St. Patrick's Day,

At Twickenham,

We beat the English in rugby to add

The Grand Slam to

The already secured Six Nations title.

I also missed Cheltenham, where Irish horses won over twenty
races.

All this with the murder of a child hanging over my head.

I don't much remember those two days as I had the mother of a hangover, ferocious guilt, remorse without the aid of booze, Xanax, even a cig.

I did learn that the boy had been hit over the head once with thundering force.

"A hurley,"

Said Sheridan.

Adding,

"Your weapon of choice, Jack, eh?"

I thought about that, asked,

"When was the lad killed?"

He sneered, said,

"You already know that, surely."

I bit down, asked,

"Humor me."

Resigned sigh from him, then,

"Eight in the evening, the day after you tossed him in the canal."

The proverbial light above my head. I did a rapid calculation and, *bingo!*

Fuck me, I had the most incredible alibi ever, hugged it close like all the rosaries I'd meant to say but never did.

Sheridan sussed the change, demanded,

"What, what is it, you have an alibi?"

I gave him the most vicious smile I had, said,

"Lawyer."

* * *

Jeremy Brett-Shaw arrived with trumpets.

Like loud.

Presence felt.

He was a short man but booming; everything about him screamed,

"Look at me."

It was hard not to.

He used his reduced stature like a sly intimidation.

Storming into my cell, roaring,

"Gather your gear, Mr. Taylor. We are so out of here."

Throwing in the American phrase to show he was *current*.

I had spoken to him very briefly on my one allowed call, enough to tell him my gold alibi and, most important, prove I could pay his outrageous fees.

He was in his late sixties and seemed like every single year had been of note.

His suit was just the biz, the kind you could throw in a ball and it would bounce right back to pristine shape, a suit that declared,

"It may have cost the earth but, I mean, just *fucking feel the quality*."

He had a well-trimmed beard, a substantial belly, tiny feet, and his hair was that salt-and-pepper style not seen since the TV show *Dynasty*.

As I shrugged into my jacket, Sheridan came blustering in, snarled,

"Who the fuck are you?"

He made the mistake of seeing Brett-Shaw's small stature as something to exploit.

Phew-oh.

Brett-Shaw drew himself up to all of his five-foot, five-inch height and the energy emanating appeared to increase his stature.

Righteous indignation has its uses.

He hissed,

"Sheridan, I believe, the so-called supercop?"

He paused as if to savor the taste of what was coming.

Continued,

"Honest to god Guards, *real cops,* are out searching for a cop killer and *you,*"

Venom dripped from his lips,

"Are instead harassing a local legend, a bona fide hero who saved the swans of Galway, *you . . .*"

He looked like he was going to spit.

Didn't, quite.

"*You,* who didn't even take the blooming time to check a rock solid alibi."

Sheridan, momentarily lost, rallied,

"Alibi? Fucking alibi? I'd bet a week's salary to hear that."

Brett-Shaw rocked back on his heels, said,

"Nun."

Sheridan was orgasmic, shouted,

"None. I fucking knew it, you sniveling ambulance chaser, none, fucking beautiful."

Brett-Shaw held out his hand, asked,

"The week's salary? All major credit cards acceptable."

Sheridan, confused, near stammered,

"But you said none."

Brett-Shaw with exaggerated care fixed the knot in his Masonic tie, said,

"Nun. My esteemed client was with a nun."

The Poor Clares are as much a part of the tapestry of Galway as the swans.

They are a secluded order,

But they've recently gone online!

Go figure.

And they have an outreach program, in the form of Sister Maeve.

A dote of a woman if such can be said of a nun without provocation.

She wasn't quite yet part of the

Me Too movement but early days.

'Tis a shame but true that in the manic years of the Celtic Tiger the bells of the Poor Clares rang out, a plea for alms.

I cringe to think they might have been hungry.

When you've been raised in and to poverty, you are keenly sensitive to the very dread of people without their dinner.

On special days, there is a Mass in the Poor Clares' convent and the public can attend. They usually have a chorister who'd make you believe in love, such is the beauty of the singing.

The church is lit with candles and has a subdued golden glow, like you'd think a medieval service might have appeared.

It is uplifting in a fashion that is just nigh on impossible to articulate.

Sister Maeve had invited me.

She was my friend.

How weird is that?

Me and the nun.

Believe that?

Years back, I had been of some small service to her and her convent—nothing trailblazing but it dazzled her and thus our unlikely friendship.

The bricks

To raise funds for a renovation to the convent, the public were invited to

"*Buy a brick.*"

To my disappointment, you didn't actually get a brick; you got a parchment saying you had donated, so I took a brick from the building site, placed a cross made from horseshoe nails on it, and that did for me.

Looked kind of a piece with the crystal skull some intruder had left for me.

So, the evening that the boy was murdered, I was singing in
the choir, so to say,

With Maeve by my side.

Afterward, I took Maeve for a drink to Garavan's.

Like a date.

Seriously?

We got the snug and I treated her to hot toddies.

She protested,

"I really shouldn't."

I said,

"'Tis the glory of it, not being the right thing."

She took a deep wallop, purred,

"Ah, that is wicked."

From a nun?

Is there higher endorsement?

The days after my daughter was murdered right before my eyes,
I was beyond

Briste.

Broken, in Irish,

But it means oh so much more,

An utter annihilation of every ounce of your beating, bedraggled heart.

And Maeve came to me

Like a vision, almost.

She fed me,
Doled out rationed amounts of Jay,
Held my trembling palms.
And, I will never quite know why,
She recited a section of what I can only term
The Jesuit poem
"The
        Wreck
                of
                    the
                        Deutschland."
Serendipity that his poem was dedicated

To the happy memory
Of five Franciscan nuns . . .
Drowned
Between midnight and morning
Of Dec. 7th, 1875.

Did Maeve select this because my daughter was born in Germany?
Or because those poor nuns were drowned?
As if reading my very thought, she intoned softly,
"Your girl is, and always will be, The Galway Girl."
Made me weep like a banshee.
Later, when I read about the poet

Gerard Manley Hopkins, I learned he was

An academic

Scholar

Poet

And fiercely unsuccessful with his poetry in his lifetime.

Now, of course, when it's of precious little value to him, they rave about him being

"One of the very greatest Victorian poets."

Fuck 'em.

Of the many odd places I end up,

The Protestant Church is unlikely to be one of them.

Not that I have a grudge against the Protestants, it's just an instinct of not belonging,

Like King Charles on the throne of England.

But here I was

In St. Nicholas.

You can see the imprints of hooves, they say, at the door, supposedly from when Christopher Columbus prayed here before setting off to find America.

They are not the devil's mark, that's for sure. He has no business here.

I sat at a back pew, found a modicum of fragile peace, my hand with the mutilated fingers found a sheet of frayed parchment.

It was a fragment of a poem by Robert Bridges,

And the title—
> Oh,
>> Sweet
>>> Jesus

That is not the title, that was my reaction to this:
"On

    a
>> Dead
>>> Child."

Phew-oh.
Riddle me that?

Perfect little body, without fault or stain on thee, . . .
Thy mother's treasure wert thou. . . .

Thy hand clasps, as 'twas wont, my finger, and holds it:
But the grasp is the clasp of death. . . .

Unwilling, alone we embark,
And the things we have seen
And have known
And have heard of

(A long pause is vital here before the killer words.)

Fail us

Here's the odd thing

I have never been entirely comfortable with the big hitters of poetry,

The

> Yeatses
>> Eliots
>>> Heaneys.

Always more in sync with the minors

> Louis MacNeice
> Anne Sexton
> Francis Thompson.

And among my dark favorites is the leader of the minor league

Totally unknown

Weldon Kees.

Could it be that in 1955, his car was found abandoned on the Golden Gate Bridge and he was never seen again, and

1951 is the year of the birth of one of the minor league mystery novelists?

Weldon's best poem is, I figured, the coincidentally titled "Crime Club."

It has these lines in the opening stanza

. . . the corpse quite dead.
The wife in Florida.

The second line seems to me to be indicative of great dry humor,
And the two-line ending is a doozy:

Screaming all day of war,
screaming that nothing can be solved.

A friend of Kees's summed up his sad life in a sentence that might well, alas, apply to my own befuddled existence:
"He was absent from his own life."
What a fucking condemnation of one man's time.

These days of hovering depression, despair, and bafflement.
I listened to Snow Patrol's new album. They had a three-year hiatus while Gary Lightbody battled the booze. He described the wait until five in the evening as he shook and suffered before he could have that drink,
A habit shared by thousands of Irish women who had that first glass of wine but not until six. He spoke of his self-loathing, sense of failure, so six months after he quit the booze he had to face the demons that drove him to drink.
The lyrics on the new album are deep, personal:
His father's dementia,
See who he was his own self.
Scary shit.

I know. I step on to that similar battleground, knowing one
battle won is but a spit in the face of the war.

And

Those bullets from a previous skirmish are useless in the next.

I reread Fred Exley's *A Fan's Notes.*

The line,

"Drink to dim the light of the world."

I need to set a dimmer my own self.

"As
  Kingfishers
          Catch
                Fire"
  Gerard Manley Hopkins

Scott finally met Jericho

And Stapleton's son.

The trio would eventually form an unholy alliance with the purpose of

Killings Guards

Causing chaos

And wreaking havoc in Jack Taylor's life.

Here's how that went down.

Jericho was a Galway girl.

When Scott killed his third Guard, a new recruit named Sullivan,

He did the deed, then darted into an alleyway.

Risky

To wait so close to the scene of the shooting, but he had to find out if the crazy girl was still on his ass.

She was.

He heard,

"Risky!"

Fuck, could she read minds?

This girl was eerily stalking him.

Why?

He leveled the gun at her, his hand displaying a more than noticeable tremor.

Was she scared?

Yeah, right.

Hand on hip, she said,

"Don't be a gobshite."

Then she snapped the weapon out of his hand in a fluid motion, said,

"I'm Trish, but you can call me Jericho. I've formed a crew"—American hard-ass inflection—"with a burglar and we both share an idea. We want to fuck with an old dude name of Jack Taylor. He killed our kin and *you, you* he witnessed killing the lady cop, so . . ."

Long pause.

"Wanna play?"

He was, as they utter in novels of merit,

Flummoxed.

Or,

As they say in Galway,

Fucked.

So she urged,

"We better like hit the road, Jack, or you'll be like the Ulster rugby players, *spit roast*."

Scott was not the most avid consumer of news. He was a beat above Kardashian but he knew that term from his stash of porn. He asked,

"What are we going to do next?"

She gave a smile of such gorgeousness that he got an instant hard-on, which she noted. She said,

"We, my not so brightest Scott, are going to send the bould Mr. Taylor some pizza. Lots and lots of pizza."

Scott was now in that state of mind described by O'Casey as "In chassis."

That in Galway we call fucked also.

So he asked the obvious.

"Why?"

She made a mock sigh as if it were self-evident, said,

"To fuck with his head. I left him a crystal skull, then stole all his mirrors."

Scott wondered if maybe it was best to try to get the gun back and just shoot the bitch.

She waved a slim finger with an inverted cross on the nail, said,

"Whoa, don't think about it. Now let's go and get wasted with Stapes."

They went to McSwiggan's as Jericho liked the tree in the lounge.

Yes, an actual tree, don't even ask.

Jericho charmed the bar guy like putty and he brought them very fine margaritas. He left his number on a beer mat. She looked at it, tossed it like a mini Frisbee, said,

"Loser."

They drank, Scott in a mind-speeding clusterfuck of emotions.

Adrenaline high from the shooting.

Mad hots for Jericho.

Utter confusion as to what the hell was going down.

The drink gave him some space and he wired down a tad, asked,

"How'd you meet Stapes?"

She was vaping from a long black shiny tube, billows of smoke hovering, and a man, uptight in general, glared at her. She said,

"Stapes was robbing my apartment."

Scott pushed,

"Did you attack him?"

"I gave him a mild scolding and a blow job."

She didn't mention that Stapes bore a resemblance to her father and that she hated her father.

The gent who'd been glaring at her could stand it no longer, marched over, snarled,

"Miss, you cannot smoke in here."

She never looked at him, said,

"'Tis vaping."

Triumphant, he blurted,

"The law treats that nonsense the same."

She stood up, grabbed the guy's crotch, hard, asked,

"That do anything for you, darlin'?"

He winced, unable to get words out. Jericho planted a tiny kiss on his neck, whispered,

"Bite me."

Outside, Jericho was on fire, her mind ablaze from the rush of the scene,
Un . . . til
Until she saw the raven on the roof of a car.
She shuddered.

* * *

Stapes, as Jericho called him, was fresh from breaking into the local church.

Sacrilege?

You betcha.

His dad, Lord rest him, had frequently intoned,

"The only good church is a desecrated one."

Man, it was a blast.

He was renting a very expensive apartment in Salthill, Ocean Towers, right across from the Blackrock Diving Tower.

But a spit, really, from Jack Taylor's gaff.

Part of the motivation.

The cost didn't bother him as he'd burgle the landlord when he split.

And dude, he, like, always legged it.

His dad's rule of thumb:

Never nest too long in any kip.

He was in love/lust/heat with Jericho.

He did think,

"Dumb-ass name."

His thoughts were an intense blend of Irish/U.S./U.K.

Mongrel mind.

He had broken into her apartment, not knowing her but convinced the place was empty. He'd been doing some lines and, in truth, his judgment was shot to shite.

He was emptying a stash of gold coins he'd found in her knickers drawer, thinking,

"Silk?"

Bang.

A shot whacked into the wall beside the press he was rifling.

Scared the bejaysus out of him.

Turned to see a fine-looking young woman, dressed in jeans, T with the slogan,

"I've got you, babe."

She was pretty in a lopsided fashion. What appeared to be a scar above her mouth should have ruined her but it added a touch of hurt that was appealing. Her hair was fade cut and jet black. She looked like . . .

Like

A fuckin' warrior.

And a slight smile hinted she was very easy with firearms.

She said,

"The fuck you doing in my knickers?"

He had never really been a guy who told the truth.

It never yielded much in benefits.

He was all about the benefits.

But something about this . . .

This chick,

As his father called them,

Unnerved him and had him try the actual truth.

He said,

"I'm a burglar, like you know, stealing your stuff."

She considered this, then racked the slide. He could hear the ratchet of the next bullet getting ready.

She said,

"So, I could like shoot you, and the law would be on my side."

He acknowledged this with a slight nod, then tried,

"But you'd never know what you missed in the sack."

She laughed, a nice dirty sound, then,

"Cheeky bugger, aren't you?"

And so it began:

Raw sex;

Violence (which they both enjoyed);

Revenge, a joint aim;

Hatred for Jack Taylor for different reasons but close enough;

A feel for chaos.

Jericho told him about being at the Burning Man festival,

Which he knew jack—no pun intended—shit about.

And meeting

The love of her crazy life:

Em/Emerald/Emily.

Becoming her lover, ally, all-round bestie.

They'd done acid at the Joshua Tree because of some weird fucked-upness of Em's about U2, and there Em had baptized her

. . . Jericho.

Emerald had called her Jericho because of a fairly bad movie but more of that later. She liked to throw in the U2 reference as it made her seem a little dim, which kept the enemy off balance, and for Jericho everyone was the enemy.

Taylor killed Em.

Taylor killed Stapes's dad.

So,

Not rocket science, they had a common motive.

They'd bring in Scott because he was already killing Guards and, mainly, his bollixed mind suited their vague general plan of *just fuck everything and have crack doing it.*

Crack in the Irish meaning of fun but they were open to dope of any hue.

Of course they were.

After a particular bout of sex, more violent than intimate, Stapes was lying back in bed. Jericho said,

"I had a sister, Gina, adored by my family."

She let out a sigh, said,

"Glorious Gina, my daddy called her."

Stapes sat up, indicated the chain around her neck, the two G's on it, figured,

"So that's the two G's, eh?"

She lashed out with ferocity. He saw the serpent that lurked behind those eyes. She hissed,

"Don't be fucking absurd."
He nearly said,
"Or maybe gone girl."
But thought she might well slit his throat—
Which is exactly the thought she was entertaining.

Emerald had said to Jericho,
    "Gather a few allies, lure them with whatever it takes,
    Then fuck them over."
Jericho, still not fully in Emerald's mind-set, asked,
    "Why?"
Emerald had given her a radiant smile, said,
    "Because it feels so good to see them burn."
Jericho had only one real fear:
    Crows, ravens, hawks.
    When she'd pushed her sister into traffic, a jet-black crow had settled on her windowsill.
    Scared the living hell out of her.
    Those beady eyes.
    At similar moments of her violent acts, of which even she'd lost count, a dark bird would appear like clockwork at her window.
    No amount of rationality could rid her of the ice freeze fear the birds inspired.
    She'd told Emerald, who didn't blow it off, but said,
    "Witchy shit."

Not that he was alone.
He also had his library, of course.
After Astrid died, he filled the void
Of words unspoken
With the new silence
Of books unread.

Derek B. Miller, *American by Day*

Ireland was gripped by three issues,

Burning ones.

1. Four Irish/Ulster rugby players, after a horrendous three-week rape trial, were found not guilty.

The girl who made the allegations was subjected to interrogation that was as vicious as it was cruel.

2. The coming referendum on abortion.

The abolition of Section 8, as it was known.

Ferocious feelings on both sides.

And daily, as No and Yes supporters clamored to be heard, you could sense a terrible violence simmering.

3. Big Tom died.

Who?

You might ask.

The godfather of Irish country music.

He was the very essence of the gentle giant.

His major hit, way back when a song meant something, was "Four Country Roads."

Put the sweet small town Glenamaddy on the minds of an older generation, the generation who would never understand Tinder, or indeed would never want to.

Tinder for the fading generation was simply something to light fires.

Of course, the new meaning set something ablaze, too, and nothing about it had a single thing to recommend it.

I met Owen Daglish in Garavan's; he looked wrecked.

I didn't think it was the right time to ask,

"How ya doing?"

Another Guard had been killed, so I went with,

"What can I get you?"

Large Jay and a pint.

Me too.

We were leaning on the counter like almost normal guys.

Popped in for a quickie after work.

That wasn't us.

Never had been,

Never would be.

We drank with little joy but fierce determination.

Owen looked fucked: red eyes, black sacks beneath, unshaven, and a vibe of rage that rose in wings above him. This was a time to tread very easy, so I went,

"Man City won the premier."

Fuck, he is a United fan, right city, wrong team.

He glared at me, near spat,

"Ah, we fuckin' handed it to them."

Should I encourage this, have a wee lad's back-and-forth about Mourinho versus Pep? But a guy in his twenties, all aglow with piss and vinegar, nearly pushed Owen aside as he barked,

"Barkeep, bottle of your best white, some clean glasses."

Silence.

Garavan's is not the pub for such shite.

Bad as it was, the guy then produced his iPhone and addressed it loudly; they're always loud, these guys.

The bar guy, Sean, not the most tolerant person, looked at the wine order, asked,

"You sure you're in the right place?"

The fellow did that quizzical face of

You for real?

Owen had had enough of this bollix practically shouting in his ear, reared back, snarled,

"Get the fuck out of my space."

The phone was put away as, get this,

The guy took a fight stance, demanded,

"You want to take this outside, asshole?"

Sean laughed in dismay, I near choked on my Jay, and Owen . . . well, Owen did what thirty years of playing hurley taught him. He did the minor swerve that is like manic choreography, and without actually moving from the counter he punched the guy fast, hard, accurate in the gut.

Then he turned to me, asked,

"Whose round?"

Many drinks later, I dared to ask,

"Did you know the Guard who was killed?"

He sighed, said,

"He's the fourth. Some fucker is on a spree. This time witnesses, who as you know are as reliable as a nun on steroids, said there were two of them, shooters I mean, and they all agree one was a woman."

He turned to me, said,

"A woman, Jesus in heaven. The world is fucked. Forty million to bring the pope here and hundreds on trolleys, a gay Indian as leader of the country telling us we have to vote yes to abortion."

These were the longest sentences he'd ever spoken. He drained his pint, said,

"To top it all, Arsène Wenger had to quit before he was fired from the Arsenal, after twenty-two years of service."

I had nothing, not even the dregs of my Jay, to stare into, so after a long silence while he reupped our drinks, he said,

"There was a note left, in Irish again, like at the first two killings. Do you want to know what it read?"

Like, hello.

Yes.

I nodded vaguely, as if I didn't mind.

I did mind.

More than I cared to admit.

He said,

"*An cailin as Gaillimh.*"

I translated,

"Galway girl."

He looked at me, a fine warm flush giving him the appearance of sunburn. He asked,

"So, Mister Private Eye, or whatever the fuck you are, what do you make of that?"

The late turn to aggression was nothing new to me. I said, as quietly, as simply, as I could,

"That she's from Galway."

Jericho had only ever shared her past with one person.

Emerald.

They'd been hitting the booze hard and Emerald suddenly handed Jericho a gold chain, two gold G's on it, said,

"For us, always, you are my golden girl."

Jericho said,

"Golden girl, how odd you should give me that.

It's what they called my sister sometimes, that or glorious."

Emerald waited, so she continued,

"She was younger than me, golden curls, face like an angel, and just so fucking cutesy pie. I was supposed to mind her. We were coming home from school, I gave her a tiny bump, and a car ran over her, and maybe a bus, too."

She took a breath, then,

"I thought, now I'll be the golden girl, but fuck, worse, they made her into some kind of saint, always young, always beautiful, never to make any mistakes, so I knew then, knew that they loved the dead and I swore I'd give them plenty to love."

Emerald laughed, fingered the two G's, said,

"The original gone girl."

"Say, are you an actor?"
"Miss, we are all actors."
She thought about this.
"I'm not," she said.
"Then," said the stranger,
His tone never varying from amused condescension,
"You're fucked."

John Connolly, *The Woman in the Woods*

Mid-April, we had three days of lovely weather, so the country bought barbecues, gallons of ice cream, sunglasses, and the beaches were thronged.

I was standing at the top of Eyre Square, a vast mass of people grabbing every spare area of grass. I'd never seen so much white skin, skin gasping for vitamin D. Gone were the days when you might have said,

"'Twas black with people."

The PC police would be all over your white arse.

A man was standing beside me, said,

"Did you see *Britain's Got Talent*?"

I knew him from somewhere and the feeling was that it had not been good.

I answered,

"No."

He continued with great excitement,

"Father Ray Kelly, sixty-four years old, he fucking blew them away with 'Everybody Hurts.'"

Father Ray was officiating at a wedding four years ago and he did a storming version of "Hallelujah." It went viral and everybody knows him.

I tried to hold back on the bitterness leaking over my reply,

"Save me."

He was not to be stopped, said,

"They're already saying he'll be the next Susan Boyle."

This was so open to a nasty line that I skipped it.

He rolled a cig: papers, pouch tobacco, the works. He did it with fluid expertise, then lit it with a large match, from the kitchen issue box.

He said,

"A fellah like that priest could do more for the Church than bringing the pope over, which will cost us forty million."

Then he gave me a curious look, said,

"You might want to buy me a drink."

I gave the look right back, said,

"I don't think so."

He gave a sly malicious laugh, said,

"I'm Amy Fadden's husband."

He tapped a foot annoyingly as he waited for me to catch up.

Amy Fadden's daughter was killed by the mayor's son; I was briefly arrested on suspicion.

I said,

"I'm very sorry for your loss, even sorrier that I didn't find any justice for your family, but with all due respect I have nothing more we can discuss."

He sneered,

With due respect.

There was something evil in his nature, and I wanted little more than to get the hell away—that, or kick him in the balls.

"Take care,"

I said, shortly.

He let me get about five steps away then near whispered,

"Amy killed him."

I followed him to Crowe's bar, the pride of Bohermore.

Ollie lined up the pints and, smart as he is, he knew this was not a drink of celebration. We took a table near the garden and watched the rain lash down, killing the heat wave. The pints settled.

I ventured,

"Lemme guess, you and your wife are not on the best of terms."

He drained half the pint, left a foam mustache,

Then he sat back, said,

"Aren't you the clever dick?"

I waited as he sank the remains of the pint, said,

"Another, and a small Paddy."

Paddy.

That's whiskey.

Not an Irishman of challenged stature, though the two have been linked on occasion.

I did.

Ollie put them on the table, muttered,

"Thanks would be nice."

And got a mocking laugh.

"So,"

I said.

"What's the story?"

He stifled a yawn, not covering his mouth, said,

"Amy hired you, knew you'd be in confrontation with the mayor's bastard son, and you did just that but, most important, in front of witnesses. Then she killed the young bollix without batting an eye but you—who could have known?—had a fucking alibi."

Pause.

"With a priest, no less."

I interjected,

"A nun."

He was aghast, asked,

"How d'you know a nun?"

I said, with all the sanctity I could muster,

"She is helping me return to the church of my youth."

This seemed to be more appalling for him to swallow than the murder of children.

I asked,

"What do you think I'm going to do about it? That's why you're here, some sort of nasty payback on your wife."

He smiled like the devil himself was proud of him, said,

"The bitch, she kicked me out of our home, that I worked for, and had the bank stop me using *our joint credit card*."

I was on my way, more out of anger than curiosity. I asked,

"I know your wife, she works for the Post Office, but you, your own self, what do you do?"

"I'm between jobs just now."

I pushed,

"Before, *before* the *between*?"

His face took on that angry riled *how dare you* expression of the fundamentally righteous. He said,

"I don't have to answer that."

I gave him my knife smile, said,

"You just did."

Leaving him, I went to feed the swans.

Sat on the bench across from the long walk where a young man had lain dead for eight months in his apartment in the city *that cared*.

We had a new cinema that cost eight million. We needed a new cinema? When two hundred people lay on trolleys in the hospital for days due to a bed shortage?

Our gay Indian government leader launched the Yes campaign, the referendum to legalize abortion.

I thought about Amy Fadden.

She'd hired me to find out who killed her daughter, and then planned to frame me for the ensuing murder of her daughter's killer.

What should I do? Which door to choose?

Revenge
Acceptance
Confrontation
Tell the Guards?
Or do what I did best:
Fuck all.
I could simply let it go.

M
A
Y
B
E.

York knows the truth
Doesn't matter in here.
Inside, the lies you tell
Become
The person you become.
On the outside, sun and reality shrink
People back to their actual size.
In here,
People grow into their
Shadows.

Rene Denfeld, The Enchanted

Jericho

Selected O'Connell's bar on Eyre Square for the first meeting of the trinity,

When she'd introduce Stapes to Scott.

Neither Scott nor Stapes knew Jericho had a lover stashed. When she'd finished with the dim duo, she'd give full attention to the one who mattered, whose heart was as black as Jericho's own.

She entered O'Connell's.

Why there of all the pubs in the city?

You'd think with her chaos fixation, her general anarchy, she'd go for a dive, some shady gig near the docks or, at the very least, some yuppie shit hole as an ironic gesture.

No.

O'Connell's over the past few years had become the *in* place for

Real estate wankers,

Budding entrepreneurs,

Billionaires on paper and by rumor (usually spread by themselves).

O'Connell's had once been an old-fashioned, very Galway pub.

Mrs. O'Connell died and financial insanity began.

Valued at eleven million in the heady, utterly mad days of the Tiger.

Get this:

She had left it to

St. Vincent de Paul.

To charity.

Many felt a cats' shelter would have made some kind of mis-guided sense.

But a charity?

Uh-oh.

And this was before the charities became as crooked publicly as the banks.

So many,

Many

Legal battles.

Jericho had no doubt that Scott, the cop killer, and Stapes, the burglar, would jell.

Why?

Because she would make it so.

She arrived first, dressed in semi-Goth, death white makeup, the kohl, biker jacket, torn jeans, and Docs.

She brought with it an air of cool that said,

"Hey, I'm out there but, like, you know, *hot*."

It worked.

The bar guy wasn't drooling but close and dared in this Me Too era to risk,

"Get cha, *babe*?"

Jericho gave him a smile and it was a winner, psycho or no. She'd that kind of smile that told you,

"*You*, you're a winner."

She ordered vodka rocks, slimline tonic.

They both enjoyed the *slimline* touch.

Scott entered next looking morose and as if he'd strayed into the wrong bar. Every bar was really the wrong one. He was just a miserable git.

Dressed in grunge but not as any statement unless

"I don't give a fuck"

Says anything at all.

He ordered a pint.

No smiles on either side of the divide.

Jericho gave him a brief nod, the one that implies,

"You have not brightened my day."

Then

Came

Mr. Bon Jovi, his own shining self.

He had his hair gelled, not overly so but sufficient that gel-less guys thought,

"Mm, maybe?"

He had a long soft leather jacket that he'd stolen and it looked either that or very expensive or, indeed, both.

He was the kind of guy who *always* knew the barman's name.

How?

Fuck knows.

Black jeans that clung to his body like a brief love and those trainers never seen much anymore.

Made by Camper.

They had a brief day in the shoe sun when Snow Patrol were *hot* and got free shoes from said company.

Those were the days of early stardom, when even Ireland was on uppers.

But then the Taylor Swift virus hit.

One of the guys got engaged to one of the *Friends* stars.

One of the women, I think.

And the lead singer did duets with everybody going the road but especially Ms. Swift. She then moved on from him to destroy all cred that Tom Hiddleston was

Enjoying after *The Night Manager*.

I am of course ashamed to be a mini version of the *National Inquirer* with all this utterly useless data but time in the dentist's office has that effect.

Scott instantly hated Stapes and it got a shade worse when Stapes greeted, effusively,

"Hiya, Sean,"

To Pavlov, the bar guy,

Who was glad of any courtesy from the Irish.

Jericho leaped to hug Stapes, and Scott thought,

"I really

Really

Hate this

Bollix."

As Jericho continued to engulf Stapes in a hug that verged on the dreaded *twerk in reverse*, if such a thing is even feasible,

Scott fumed, muttered,

"Get a friggin' room."

Jericho disengaged slowly, went,

"Phew-oh, that was intense."

Stapes put out his hand, greeted,

"You must be the infamous Scott."

Scott tried to rein in his bile but he was fucked if he'd shake hands. He said,

"You're the incompetent burglar."

Lame, right?

Sean/Pavlov, acting on a false sense of civility, brought a creamy pint, put it in Stapes's hand, said,

"On the house."

You see how insincerity gets a bad press when it can do all kinds of significant shite. Just ask the pope.

"My man,"

Said Stapes.

Jericho suggested they all sit and get the party cooking.

She began,

"Now we all know each other, let's plan our first event."

Scott, still sulking, sneered,

"Why are we trusting this loser, this failed housebreaker? We know nothing about him."

Jericho leaned over, right in Scott's face, almost like a caress, sensually whispered,

"Because I am fucking him, like biblically."

Scott pulled back as if he'd been slapped. Stapes sank most of his pint.

Jericho stood up, ordered Scott,

"Outside, now."

He slunk after her, torn between raging lust and outright hatred.

On the curb, Jericho produced a pack of Marlboro Red, shook two out, and then handed one to Scott with a slimline Zippo, said,

"Fire us up, love."

He was shaking from temper, snarled,

"I quit."

She laughed, asked,

"Smoking or our enterprise? Don't forget, I have you on video."

His shoulders sagged and he lit both cigs, offered one. She said,

"Put it in my mouth. You know you want to."

But a flash of himself shooting Guards jumped into his vision. His battered psyche cooed,

"You're better than this shite."

He asked,

"You remember you told me how you and your *best bud* bonded at that festival and that due to peyote and U2 she called you *Jericho*?"

She was cautious, not sure if the balance of power was on thin ice, tried a slow,

"Yeah, so?"

He sneered triumphantly, said,

"*The Joshua Tree* was the album."

Then, with a sneer, demanded,

"So why didn't she call you Joshua?"

He wanted to add,

"Yah dumb cunt."

But, you know, he thought,

Enough already.

Jericho nearly told him about the real reason Em called her Jericho but decided, fuck him.

He was wearing his now customary Barbour coat, one of those so worn that not a trace of wax remained. Much favored by the royals, it suggested that the wearer had good taste to begin with but years of shooting pheasant (or perhaps Guards?) had taken their cultural toll. No question of rewaxing it, as, like, that's what *the poor folk* might do.

Jericho suddenly reached out, pulled at the cargo pocket of his right leg, and in an instant grabbed the revolver.

She said, in down-home Brooklynese,

"Yah packing heat, you dumb schmuck."

She checked the cylinder, said,

"Running a little low there, Rich."

She pushed the gun into her waistband, said,

"It's been fun but thirsty work. I could *murder* a shot."

She walked rapidly back into the pub, sat, Stapes looking a tad confused. Scott followed, sat in a cloud of unknowing. Stapes said,

"Gee, guys, this little triangle is falling apart. Maybe it's time to call time."

Jericho gave them both a long look, then said,

"Let's get some shots in."

Stood, walked to the counter, shot Sean/Pavlov in the face, turned to the guys, asked,

"Who's next?"

Later, in bed with her lover, Jericho relayed the events, said,

"It was so hot. The two dudes were literally shitting their pants."

Her lover, keen to get in on the action, asked,

"When do I get to play?"

Jericho smiled, said,

"Lemme just fuck with those two, then we can begin our serious game."

"Get mad, get even, and get paid.
(What kind of loser stops
          At getting even?)"

Aidan Truhen

Jericho accompanied Scott when they shot the fourth Guard, a new recruit on traffic duty.

Jericho left a note.

Said to Scott,

"That's it for leaving notes, they're like so lame."

In the past decade there have been some horrific scandals that rocked the land:

The Magdalen laundries,

The Tuam babies,

The bankers.

But even these horrors were paling against the cervical cancer cover-up.

It blew open when a young woman who'd insisted she was not happy about her smear tests took a High Court action that revealed the HSE had known she was fatally ill for three years and hid it.

Fucking hid it.

When the woman discovered that she had only months to live, it emerged that the tests had been outsourced to a U.S. company and guess who had shares in said company?

The head of the HSE.

An arrogant bollix who, when confronted about possibly hundreds of other women who were fatally ill and had not been told, stonewalled and then announced he was soon to resign with a huge pension, but—

And here's the but—

He would devote the remainder of his time to investigating how this could have happened.

Then he went on leave, piled-up days that he was due already.

The leader of the government insisted he had full confidence in him, then returned to urging the country to vote yes and legalize abortion.

You tried to digest this utter . . . disgrace . . . and wondered

Not why we drank but why we weren't drinking lights out.

Amy Fadden, whose daughter was murdered and who tried to frame me for the killing of her daughter's killer, was enjoying cocktails in the Radisson when I caught up with her.

The Radisson was a popular venue on Fridays when they had a special cocktail hour; ladies of a certain hue, i.e., money and fuck all else to do, attended regularly. The barman looked like an escapee from Chippendales,

Hired less for his skill than his ability to fill a near see-through shirt with finesse.

I spotted Amy in, dare I say, high spirits with a table of women who looked like money was not of any pressing concern. I approached the guy, asked for a pint.

He frowned, making his chiseled looks a shade empty, and said in that new mid-Atlantic drawl,

"Perhaps Sir might be more comfortable in a more traditional setting."

I enjoyed that.

I asked,

"Are you familiar with the *traditional puck*?"

No.

He asked,

"Is it a cocktail?"

I said,

"It's a fairly fast heavy wallop to the face."

He poured the pint, said,

"Twelve euros."

Like fuck.

I said,

"See Mrs. Fadden?"

"Indeed, a valued addition to our little soirees."

I said,

"Stick it on her tab."

I strolled over to the table where the ladies were deep in drink, the table a riot of color, every conceivable brand of cocktail, tiny umbrellas, fruit wedges.

Lurking from every glass, it looked like a Dalí piss-up.

Into the middle of this Technicolor mess I plonked my ugly black pint. It appeared like a shout.

One of the ladies, her eyes a tad the worse for wear, barked,

"Excuse me!"

I nodded at Amy, said,

"How's it going, Amy?"

The others stared at her but she had nothing, so I said,

"Amy hired me to find who killed her daughter."

That threw a somber note.

A lady to my left touched my arm, asked,

"And did you?"

I leaned over, took my pint, drank noisily, belched, said,

"Amy decided to frame me for it."

Now there was utter silence.

All eyes on the bould Amy.

She rallied, said,

"It was all a terrible misunderstanding. Grief had me not knowing what was going on."

There was a slight shift in orientation as two ladies moved a tiny distance from her. I said,

"But hey, all water under the bridge,

Like the mayor's dead son.

But the good news, like a fine cocktail, is at the bottom.

You want to tell them, Amy, or will I? We found the killer of her daughter and guess what."

Long pause, then,

"Amy killed him."

Murmurings.

The lady to my left asked,

"*Killed him?*"

I looked at Amy, who seemed to have gone into a kind of toxic shock or else it was just the booze hitting hard.

I said, very clearly,

"Amy killed the boy."

They all turned to Amy who was still as a prayer lost in translation.

I stood up, said,

"I'll leave you ladies to your cocktails."

I'd reached the bar and the bar guy glared at me. I asked him,

"You heard about the barman who was shot?"

He had decided to somehow find his balls while I'd been chatting with the ladies, snarled,

"So?"

Not a whole lot of sympathy there.

I added,

"By all accounts he was a nice guy."

He shrugged, dismissing me, so I asked,

"Imagine what would happen to an asshole behind a bar?"

Duchess

Jessica

Selwyn

Rose

Over the years, I have had an embattled link to a priest.

Father Malachy.

A chain-smoking chancer who'd been my bitch mother's pet priest.

Back in those days, pious women believed it enhanced their status to have a priest in thrall; nowadays it would be a downright crime.

I'd managed to save him from various scandals, trouble over the years—not from friendship but he had a knack of inveigling me to assist him, despite his continuous loathing of me.

You might describe it as a wholly Irish connection, certainly not *holy*, unless you implied a disgrace.

Few years back I had gotten hold of a notorious *Red Book* that the Church was anxious to suppress.

Malachy, in some new bother, persuaded me to give him the book, to redeem himself in the eyes of Mother Church.

Did it ever.

He was feted, celebrated, and was now bishop-in-waiting.

Was he grateful?

Was he fuck.

Did he acknowledge my help?

Guess.

So when I saw him leaning against a black BMW outside my apartment I was not happy. He was not smoking but otherwise had the same furtive air of the new clergy.

He greeted,

"Where the hell have you been, Taylor?"

I gave him my granite look, asked,

"You the bishop yet?"

He indicated my apartment, asked,

"Can we talk?"

He gave some instructions to the driver, who drove off. I said,

"Nice to be chauffeured."

He snarled,

"He's a cheeky bollix is what he is. Asked me not to smoke in the car."

I had no sane answer to this.

We got inside. He plonked himself down on the sofa, asked,

"Jameson, no ice."

He was such a cunt that it made me laugh, so I obliged. He smelled the glass, asked,

"You sure this is Irish?"

I asked,

"Would I lie to a priest?"

He waved that away, looked round, said,

"Bit of a dump."

I said,

"'Tis penance."

He smiled grimly, said,

"God knows you have enough sins for a parish."

Then he pulled out a crumpled pack of Major, the strongest cig on the market, lit up, blew a near perfect smoke ring.

I asked,

"The point of your visit?"

He shifted, the sofa creaking under his weight as he flicked ash on what passed for carpet.

He clocked I wasn't drinking, asked,

"Nothing for you?"

I gave him what I hoped was the current clerical smile, guile with a glint, said,

"Gave it up for the souls in Purgatory."

He sneered, then snapped,

"You're probably on drugs. Your sainted mother often said, 'That pup is in on drugs.'"

I laughed, my beatific mom, who swallowed Valium like her daily intake of bile. He continued,

"She hoped and indeed prayed you'd die young."

Jesus.

I said,

"Lovely as this little chat is, is there a point?"

He seemed to sag and then, as if he had to drag it from the depths, near whispered,

"I have a sister."

He said it in the tone of a man who might say,

"I've only a day to live."

He looked at me but I had, well, nothing, so he continued.

"Jessica Selwyn, you might have heard of her. She played the duchess in that U.S. version of *Downton*, made a shit pile of money and is now here in Galway."

I asked,

"All sounds great. You must be proud."

He roared,

"I'm fucking mortified."

Oh.

He added,

"She's a bloody head case."

I countered,

"But a rich one helps a bit?"

He glared at me, said,

"You need to pay attention, she's got a . . ."

He searched for a description.

"Young lover."

I could see his bishop aspirations might be compromised, so I said,

"Not great for the image."

He was wallowing in rage and spite, said,

"Doing interviews with her arm draped around who she calls her *Galway girl*."

I'll admit it took a moment for me to grasp the word and I echoed slowly,

"Girl?"

He was so enraged froth was leaking from the corners of his mouth. He shouted,

"Carpet biters. Not only is my sister a *lesbian* but she's a cougar or whatever they call these oul wans who have young . . ."

Again, the hesitation as he reached for a word, then,

"Lovers."

Truly nearly choked him.

Did I feel for him?

No.

I asked,

"Isn't the Church into acceptance and all sorts of fake liberal shite?"

He said,

"There's that royal family thinking they have problems with the young lad marrying a black wan."

Before I could get over Malachy being a *royal watcher*, he said,

"And the country's going to legalize killing babies."

I said to him,

"You once told me when I was in deep shite that I should pray for all parties."

He looked at me in utter astonishment, said,

"Fuck that."

He stood, crushed a butt under his clerical shoe, said,

"So I can rely on you, then?"

I asked,

"For what?"

He was annoyed, said,

"To fix it."

"Fix it how?"

He muttered,

"Lord give me strength."

Then,

"To get rid of the girl."

By God, I was going to make him spell it out. I asked,

"Like kill her?"

He blessed himself, about as hypocritical an action as I've witnessed.

Said,

"God strike you mute, Taylor, for such a thought. Do one of those sly underhand things you're famous for."

Then he gave me his sister's address, warned,

"You never met me."

Right.

I asked,

"And the girl, the temptress, who is she?"

He spat the name.

"Calls herself Jericho."

"We do have a zeal for laughter
In most situations—
Give or take a dentist."

Joseph Heller

Stapleton never knew that from the moment Jericho set eyes on him, he reminded her of her father and, there and then, she signed his death warrant but, first, she'd play with him.

"Play," her daddy used to say, was so important to his girls.

Scott and Jericho were sitting in Scott's house, and it was looking more than a little run-down. Scott was bemoaning his dwindling supply of bullets.

Jericho was rapidly losing any zeal for him.

Sure, it had been a rush with a guy who just went out and shot cops.

But he was a dour miserable bollix.

Jericho asked,

"You ever think of actually cleaning?"

He looked up, genuinely puzzled, asked,

"Why?"

God in heaven.

She said,

"It's a kip."

He thought about that, then,

"Why are you shacked up with that old actress?"

Jericho sighed, said,

"One, her house is clean. She's rich, it's the perfect hideaway, but mainly it's like none of your fucking business."

He stood up, holding the gun idly in his left hand. He tried to joke,

"Is it smart to diss a guy with a gun?"

She waved a hand, said,

"One less bullet, then."

He didn't know how to deal with her and for a moment relished the thought of just shooting her, see how the bitch registered that, but she had a hold on him and he was now afraid of being alone, alone with dwindling ammunition. He asked,

"Where is our burglar?"

Jericho brightened up, a fact not missed by Scott. She said,

"He's out earning. Something you could think about."

Scott was counting his few bullets, whined,

"I'm missing one."

Jericho gave a smug smile, said,

"I, um, lent it to Stapes."

Before he could answer, she added,

"He doesn't know I did."

Stapes regarded himself as an artist.

Burglar, if you wanted to be crass,

But a class act.

Okay, okay, he'd been caught but, come on, pure bad luck and, hey, he'd learned.

His first stint in prison had been traumatic but educational. He'd celled with one of the so-called master burglars.

True, he was serving a lengthy stretch so *master* might be a little bit of a misnomer, but he could sure talk the craft. Used to intone,

1. Work alone (like *duh*).
2. Prepare, prepare, prepare.
3. Don't splash the cash.

His big talk was the . . .

Drumroll.

The big score.

Stapes might well have come to this conclusion his own self, but you cell with a guy, you really want to be critical, so he listened,

Like this:

Pass on the usual Micky Mouse shit, wait, research, and then give your all to the one.

When Stapes was leaving, he said to the master,

"You should give one of them TED Talks."

"Who's Ted?"

Stapes had the new target lined up.

Meaning, he paid a guy for the info, a guy Jericho had introduced him to.

The target was

A large home behind the golf club, nicely secluded,

Rumored to have a legendary painting by Jack B. Yeats,

The Galway Tinkers.

Denied to exist by all the experts.

But if it did . . .

Phew-oh.

Stapes's new source said in a hushed tone,

"You get that, I'll give you fifty large right then and there and a percentage of the final sale."

Fuck.

Like, really?

This particular fence owed a debt to Jericho. This was his way out of the debt, convince Stapes to burgle the house. The fence didn't ask why. He'd seen Jericho in action and it wasn't pretty.

Stapes had done his recon.

The occupiers, a couple in their late sixties, played bridge on Wednesday evenings, from seven to nine, so he duly prepared.

Black tracksuit,

Watch cap that pulled down neatly over the face but frigging inclined to heat up,

Large non-logo rucksack,

Surgical gloves.

No weapons.

(Caught with a weapon, add a fast ten to the sentence but, hey, who was getting caught?)

No negative waves.

Dwell on speed.

As he did a last-minute check on his gear, he was assailed by the image of Jericho shooting the barman in the face.

Fuck.

Brutal and beyond belief.

He sat transfixed as she calmly turned to him and Scott, the gun still smoking, and he was sure she was on a spree.

But something flicked across her face and she snapped back to whatever passed for normal in her bizarre world.

There and then Stapes knew:

"She will kill us all, sooner or later."

And he was done with those crazy fucks.

Focus.

On job in hand.

When he had his cash he'd be in the wind.

Jack Taylor? Jericho had him in her sights so he could simply let her deal with him. He did two fast lines of coke, got the ambience, then moved to boogie.

Getting into the house was so easy he was almost spooked. When it was this simple, he worried.

Moved along the ground floor to the main room and stood back, let out a

Whoosh.

The whole back wall was a mass of paintings, must be close to a hundred.

All framed but not, alas, labeled. He stood for a moment before what seemed a tornado of color, thought,

"Who the fuck is Yeats?"

Took a deep breath, muttered,

"Chill, chill, dude."

And thanked God for iPhones.

Used the phone to view the picture his source had provided, the source insisting,

"This is from a facsimile as no one has ever seen the actual painting."

Stapes had wondered,

"The fuck is a facsimile?"

Phone in one hand, he moved along the rows and lines of paintings, the colors starting to blend and whirl, giving him the beginnings of a hard-core headache. He paused.

"Step back, focus."

And did a wee bit more coke.

The icy dribble down his throat, then he exclaimed,

"Hold the bloody phones."

Bent down and, there in the left-hand corner, bingo.

His first thought was,

"Are they fucking kidding?"

To him it seemed like a kid's first attempt at stick figures. He rechecked the phone image, shrugged, muttered,

"The fuck do I know?"

Ripped it from the wall, the coke adding a degree of ferocity that brought plaster and noise.

"Whoops,"

He cried,

Now beginning to have himself a time.

He shoved it into his ruck, then considered snatching half a dozen at random but the weight alone might make it just a tired exercise in futility.

His innate greed wanted to ransack the house but, if his source was right, he already had the prize.

He was well pleased as he headed for the back door, hummed a Pogues tune, no easy feat, and opened the door.

To a sea of blue.

Stapes sat in the interrogation room of the Garda station,

His head still reeling from the utter shock of the wave of Guards waiting outside for him.

He could make no sense of it at all.

He was let stew for hours until the door opened and a plain-clothes cop walked in, a shit-eating grin on display. He said,

"I'm Sheridan. That's like the top honcho around here."

Stapes was further unnerved by the sheer confidence of the guy. This was not going to be one of those *get to spill* gigs.

This was done and dusted. He was fucked and they weren't making any attempt to hide their glee. For some bizarre reason, Stapes tried to summon up what he could of legal dramas on TV. Yeah, that desperate. He asked,

"I want a drink, a phone call, and a lawyer."

Felt he showed a small amount of hard in there.

Sheridan laughed, said,

"That's priceless, love it."

KEN BRUEN

He leaned across the chair, whispered,

"Tell you what, even though it's a huge breach of protocol, I feel today I can risk it."

Stapes felt a mad stirring of unholy hope and it increased as Sheridan produced a pack of Marlboros. Stapes near wept. A cig would be just freaking near perfect now. He muttered,

"Oh, thank you."

Sheridan looked puzzled as he withdrew a cig, lit up, inhaled deeply, asked,

"For what?"

Stapes indicated the cigs with what was now a trembling hand.

Sheridan laughed again, a laugh deepened by the nicotine, exclaimed,

"For you, your days of getting anything, any fucking thing, are so over."

Stapes whined.

"Why?"

Sheridan leaned back, blew a smoke ring at the ceiling, said,

"Shite, you really don't get it."

Stapes, in a state of near collapse, screamed,

"Get what?"

Sheridan sat up straight, said,

"We got a call that the Guard killer was hiding out where we found you and there you were."

Stapes was incredulous, screeched,

"But that's insane."

Sheridan gave him a smile of faux warmth, said,

"Bottom of your bag, we found a bullet and, for your sake, we did a rush forensics, and guess what?"

Stapes was truly lost for a reply, so Sheridan said,

"'Tis a match."

Waited.

Then,

"So, every which way, you are absolutely fucked."

Stapes tried,

"I was there to get a Jack B. Yeats. You can check, it's in the bag."

Sheridan sneered.

"That piece of shite? It's not even close to a decent copy."

As a last resort, Stapes tried,

"It's a setup. The bullet was planted."

Sheridan stood, stretched, said,

"Cop killers, phew, they get the very special treatment, so get ready for suck city."

When Jericho heard that Stapes was in custody she sighed. She would have really loved to see his face when he walked out to the sea of blue.

Now just Taylor remained.

As for Scott, she had such little regard for him that she didn't even bother setting him up.

The grand theatrical event she was planning was almost ready.

As she relished the sheer audacity and cold-bloodedness of what

Was coming, she let out a mighty cry of,
"Shock and awe."
Did glance at the window and recoiled in terror.
A large black crow was pecking at the glass, its dead eyes riveted
on her.

In the dying weeks of May 2018,
  Ireland voted by 70 percent to 30 percent in favor of legalizing abortion,
    One of the few remaining countries where it had been illegal.
    Wild celebrations with women sporting *Repeal*
    On sweatshirts.
    A man with a Down syndrome child wore his own sweatshirt.
    It read,
    Repent.

Not even sure why I agreed to help Father Malachy with the issue of his sister.
  Curiosity, mostly, to see what on earth a sister of his was like.
  She lived in a huge house off Grattan Road. No trouble identifying her home as a large plaque proclaimed
            Duchess
                Jessica
                    Selwyn
                        Rose

Obviously, modesty wasn't a problem for her.

I said to myself,

"All you have to do is persuade her young companion to leave."

Piece of cake.

Rang the doorbell and fuck, it sounded like the gong used back in the day by the Rank Organisation. The door swung open and a young woman in cut-off denim shorts, black T, bare feet, asked,

"Yeah?"

She was pretty in a haphazard way but something in her look suggested ugliness, plus she seemed to have a smirk.

I said,

"I'm here to see Ms. Rose."

She considered that, then said,

"No."

And slammed the door.

I banged the door, the fucking gong again, and the door opened. She asked,

"What?"

As if she'd never seen me before.

I put my foot in the door, snarled,

"You look familiar."

She was saved from answering by a cry from inside.

"Who is it, dear?"

I pushed by, entered a marble hall, saw a large sitting room to my left, and turned in there.

KEN BRUEN

An elderly woman, dressed in what appeared to be a Barbara Cartland / Shirley MacLaine / Fionnula Flanagan medley outfit, i.e.,

Swaths of scarves,

Bangles,

Big hair,

Gold kimono / dressing gown.

Her face had been lifted so she appeared expressionless. She purred,

"Who *have* we here?"

A wave of patchouli engulfed me. I said,

"Jack Taylor, a friend of your brother's."

She gave a massive roar, which I realized was actually a laugh, but her face didn't move. She said,

"Don't be ridiculous. My brother has no friends."

Argue that.

The girl had moved in to stand too close to my back. I turned, said,

"Rein it in."

The woman said,

"You may call me Jess."

Fuck, lucky me.

I said,

"Jess, Malachy was concerned about your welfare."

The girl snorted.

Jess said,

"My intern PA with the intriguing name Jericho is very protective of me."

I said,

"That's sweet but I need a word in private."

Jericho moved next to Jess. Didn't quite sit in her lap but was in the neighborhood. Jess said,

"We have no secrets in this house. That's the sort of thing Malachy and his cronies indulge in."

Dilemma.

How to delicately say,

Get shot of the girl,

Fire her,

Kick her arse out.

I said,

"Get rid of the girl."

They both gasped as if they had rehearsed and maybe they had. Jericho said,

"Don't let the door hit you in the ass on your way out."

I tried,

"I'll leave my number, if you want to talk."

Jericho moved up real close to me, said,

"Fuck off."

I gave her my benign face, said,

"We'll meet again."

She sneered, said,

"Count on it."

Psychopaths are distinguished by two characteristics. The first is ruthless disregard for others; they will defraud, maim, and kill for the most trivial gain. The second is an astonishing gift for disguising the first. It's the deception that makes them so dangerous. You never see them coming.

It is said that childhood forms utterly who we are.

There is no escape.

In Jericho's home, one room at the top of the house was off-limits to Jericho and her young sister, Gina; it supposedly held a priceless picture by Jack B. Yeats.

Jericho, despite dire warnings, went into the room. A huge skylight illuminated a portrait on the wall.

Jericho was startled when a raven came through the window and was trapped. It flew crazily,

Crashing into walls.

Jericho was screaming when Gina turned the key in the door, locking her in with the raven.

Hours later, her father managed to open the door. He found Jericho unconscious on the floor, the painting ripped from the wall and in shreds,

And the savagely torn remains of a raven.

Pieces of the bird were lodged in the girl's teeth and a piece of the frame was shoved through the raven's eyes.

Jericho absolutely blanked this event from her memory; she never connected it to the push she gave to Gina into traffic.

Nor did her intermittent shudder at the sight of a raven dredge up the memory, so deeply was it buried.

She did develop a fixation on the painter Jack B. Yeats.

Roseanne Barr,

In a series of twenty-four-hour tweets, scuppered her new show,

Letting loose a rant of monstrous bile.

Later, in an attempt at justification, she blamed the sleeping aid Ativan.

The makers, in a memorable response, admitted,

"Indeed, our product does have some side effects, but

We didn't realize it included racism."

From nowhere, we got another ten days of sweltering heat wave.

Joy indeed,

But—

In Ireland, we always include the *but*—

Humidity.

The fuck we know about humidity?

Left us with a dilemma:

We daren't complain about the heat, God forbid, you may as well diss the pope, but this wet, corrosive temperature did fray nerves.

We muttered,

"Grand weather."

As rivers of sweat immersed us.

Sheridan, the supercop, joined me as I had a pint in Garavan's. He was dressed in a light linen shirt, already creased in the heat, and shorts. Sunglasses propped on his head, he ordered an iced tea.

The bar guy stared at him, asked,

"You do know this is a pub?"

Sheridan, never noted for his patience, snapped,

"Give me a very ice cold Coke then."

Got that and rolled the bottle across his forehead, said,

"Phew, that's better."

I was wearing a T with cooling material, light fawn jeans, and, have to say, looked like this weather was no surprise to me.

He was kind of impressed, said.

"Cool guy."

I nodded, said,

"We have our moments."

He let me savor that, then said,

"Hate to rain on your coolness."

"But you will."

He drained the Coke bottle, making a spectacle of it, then,

"You know we have the Guard killer?"

I did, and was astonished they were charging Stapleton, but I went with,

"Alleged, surely. Alleged killer."

He gave a wry chuckle, said,

"We have, literally, the burning bullet."

I had nothing to add, so he pushed,

"But here's the best bit . . ."

And he waited.

I ordered a round, no intention of playing his game, so he caved, said,

"He wants to see you."

"No,"

I said.

Sheridan was still in the flush of mind fucking, said,

"He promises to deliver the *real* killer if you go to see him."

I looked at him, asked,

"Are you asking for my help?"

He mulled that, then,

"Not really *asking*. Think if it as a veiled threat."

"*Veiled?* Sounds almost benign."

He snarled.

"It's anything but fucking benign."

Stapleton looked more than the worse for wear when I visited him. We were in the *green* room, so named not because of its hospitality but rather to imply intimidation.

Puke green.

Stapes had a complexion to match and a dark bruise under his left eye. He also appeared to have lost some teeth and a lot of weight.

The smart-arse cocky fuck I'd met before was long gone. A Guard who weighed at least 320 pounds sat on a chair very close to us. He was reading the *Daily Mirror*. I swear, his lips were moving as he perused the sports page. I asked,

"Could you back it up a bit, some privacy maybe?"

He looked at me with deep hatred, said,

"He's a cop killer."

I said,

"So that's a no?"

He put down the paper, recognition lit his face, said,

"I know you."

This would not, I felt, be to our advantage.

I tried,

"Good to see you."

He got to his feet, said,

"You used to be a Guard. What are you doing talking to this piece of shite?"

I said,

"He might be innocent."

He sat back down, glanced at the wall clock, said,

"You have five more minutes."

I could have argued but let it slide. The guy added,

"Children keep getting killed around you."

Did it piss me off, incline me to action?

I bit down, looked at Stapes, asked,

"What's the story?"

In a low whisper, he told me about:

Scott

Jericho

Even the barman being shot.

I asked,

"You were part of all this?"

Searched for a term, tried,

"You were part of this *gang*?"

He rolled his eyes, managed to actually sound offended, said,

"Man, for fuck's sake, I was playing along until I could call the cops."

Before I could pour scorn on this, he added,

"That's why they set me up."

I sat trying to take all this in, then stood up.

He asked,

"What do you think?

"I think you are completely fucked."

It wasn't hard to track Scott down.

His father had been a supercop and Scott, not exactly following the family biz, did two years in jail.

He lived in the family home, off Taylor's Hill, the posh side of town—or used to be. I broke in early in the morning, figuring Scott wasn't a guy to be up doing chores.

He wasn't.

The house had indeed once been grand but was now threadbare, anything of value sold. I went quietly up a fine old staircase, found Scott snoring loudly in what seemed like the master bedroom.

Empty bottles scattered all round, and discarded clothes.

A minimum of searching revealed the gun; it held one bullet.

I pulled up a chair beside his bed, settled myself, then kicked the bed, hard, repeatedly. His face contorted in fright, he looked at me, the gun, muttered,

"Oh, fuck."

I let him hear the cylinder click, said,

"Stapes sent me."

Horror ran across his face like the prayers you knew were never going to be answered. He looked around for help, there was none, so he asked,

"Are you going to kill me?"

I said,

"I think so."

He cried.

I mean, he really bawled.

The author Jilly Cooper recently asked,

"What is it with new men, they're always weeping."

Mind you, a gun in your face could be a good excuse.

When that subsided, he asked,

"Can I put on a T-shirt, some jeans?"

Did that with trembling fingers. His T had the logo

Women Are the New Black.

Cute.

Sensing I might be relenting, he pushed,

"Can I, like, get a shot of booze?"

I slapped him twice upside the head, hard.

Dazed, he whined,

"What'd you do that for?"

I asked,

"Why'd you kill the Guards?"

I think he told the truth, said,

"To get back at my father."

I found his bottle of Southern Comfort, let him have a glass, and the effect was near instant. He sat up straight, said,

"I'll tell you about Jericho if you don't kill me."

She was, he said,

"My soul mate."

I sighed, indicated he continue.

Jericho was planning on getting rid of the old actress, taking the house, killing Jack Taylor as he was responsible for the death of Emerald, her soul sister.

(Lots of soul shit, I thought.)

But,

Stapleton had fucked everything up by sleeping with Jericho, then Jericho, tired of him, set him up.

I reached into my jacket, clicked off the recorder.

Scott stared at me in horror and, get this, betrayal, whined,

"You recorded this."

I stood up, said,

"You have a choice."

Tears again, God almighty. He asked,

"What?"

"Run or turn yourself in."

I stood up, put the gun in my jacket. He asked,

"How am I going to defend myself?"

I said,

"Try foul language."

Deargar:
A carnival of bloodshed.

There is a term in psychology,
A chilling one.
"The theater of murder."
Jericho loved this.
She didn't need it explained.
She knew how to murder with the maximum of drama.

There is a tinker woman named Brid I meet at odd times. She is supposed to have the *bronntanas*, the gift of seeing.

Certainly, there have been times when she foretold events in my life that proved to be all too tragically true.

Do I believe it?

Phew-oh. When you have been raised a guilt-ridden Catholic, with a native tongue awash in curses, prophecies, banshees, the odd leprechaun, you tend to keep, if not an open mind, then certainly options open.

After I left Scott, with the damning recording in my jacket, I met her in Buttermilk Lane, our version of the Yellow Brick Road.

She wore the handwoven Connemara shawl, a riot of rings and bangles, and she could have been anything from fifty to seventy, with a ton of hair, long, jet-black, and always immaculately washed, with a scent of roses.

Her eyes, a washed-out nigh white with flecks of what ofttimes seemed to shine gold that I told myself was a trick of the light.

"Young Taylor,"

She said.

Insofar as I could gauge, she had a certain fondness for me, thanks to some assistance I had rendered to her people. I instinctively knew that was the smart place to be with her. Once, I had seen her wrath when a group of young trainee thugs had called her names.

She had unleashed a torrent of curses that seemed to frighten the shite out of them and they cowered away, like beaten dogs.

I put in her hand a mess of notes, which she quickly hid in her shawl, then she took my hand and closed her eyes.

She swayed from side to side, my hand held tight, then muttered,

"*Och ocon.*"

This is not good.

Means,

"Woe is me."

And a whole slew of other shite too, none if it good.

She said,

"*Bhi curamach leis an cailin Gaillimh.*"

"Beware the Galway girl."

Added,

"*An deargar ag teacht.*"

"The bloodletting is coming."

Then she reached beneath her shawl, took out a tied piece of leather with a small stone cross, put it around my neck, said,

182

"*Bheannacht leat.*"

"Bless you."

Then she was gone and, like the narrator of the poem by Padraig Pearse,

I was left wondering.

Some months later, I was walking through the Galway market. A guy from Lithuania was selling a whole row of exactly the same item.

I asked, hoping that maybe Brid had a small cottage industry going, where he got them. He said,

"We import them from China."

Scott, after I left, looked out the window, saw two suited men approaching his door, ran to the roof and, in utter silence, threw himself off.

The men were Jehovah's Witnesses.

Amy Fadden, mother of the girl who had been murdered, waited patiently for the bus that normally took her daughter to school. As it accelerated to turn from the roundabout, she stepped in front of it.

Her estranged husband, drinking a combo of brandy and cheap wine, suffocated on his own vomit.

Did the above qualify as the *bloodletting*?

I had given the recording of Scott to Owen Daglish, expecting
    1. Stapes would be released.

2. Jericho would be arrested.

Despite my years of experience to the contrary I thought justice would prevail.

Bollocks.

Here's what happened:

Stapes was charged with aggravated burglary and as a co-conspirator in the Guards killings.

Jericho would not be charged. Hearsay from the recording of a dead man was not evidence.

Daglish quipped,

"See, a burglar in the nick is worth two in the wind."

I said to Daglish,

"This is such bullshit."

He smiled, said,

"No, simply Galway."

How to succeed in Galway
Without really trying:

1. Drink in O'Connell's bar on Eyre Square.
2. Have three interchangeable shirts—
   a. Galway Hurling shirt
   b. Connacht Rugby shirt
   c. Galway United shirt
3. Marry a Galway girl.

Father Malachy's sister,

The Duchess Jess—

I had to talk to her without Jericho around.

So I sat outside the house, waited.

Round noon, Jericho appeared with, from her demeanor, not a care in the world. She got into a dark Audi, no doubt belonging to Jess, drove off like a woman who had the world by the balls.

I was dressed in semi-respectable mode: even a Masonic tie I'd beaten off a Mason, the jacket of my funeral suit, near white shirt, 501s and the Docs with the closest thing to a sheen on them there'd ever be.

I had the look of a failed accountant who moonlighted as a morgue attendant.

I knocked on the door, waited.

Took five minutes, then the door opened to Jess.

Jess, reeking of gin and a powerhouse perfume, the make-you-gag type.

She was dressed in what seemed to be the curtains from the Abbey Theatre. She nigh whispered,

"Have you come to fix the TV?"

I said,

"Malachy sent me."

Seemed to take a moment for her to recall who he was, then,

"Weren't you here before?"

"Yes. Might I have a word?"

As she hesitated, I added,

"I might be able to fix the TV."

I was in.

She draped herself on what theatrical people refer to as a *chaise longue*.

Ordered,

"Pour us some drinkies, like a good man."

I poured her a sizable gin, asked,

"Ice?"

Got,

"You silly man."

So, no, then.

I allowed myself a single malt, like a character in a serious novel, sat opposite her, waited.

She demolished the drink, asked,

"Who are you again?"

"Jack Taylor."

I laid out the whole sorry story of Scott, Stapes, and the lethal Jericho. Took a while and I think she dozed. When I was done, I took her glass, filled it with tonic, handed it over, said,

"So, bottom line, Jericho is going to kill you."

She seemed to ponder this, then,

"Are you married?"

I said,

"I was."

This seemed to please her and she asked,

"Couldn't cut it, huh?"

I tried again to get her attention.

"Your little house pet, roommate, is going to kill you."

She made an effort to stand, motioning me to leave, said,

"I tire of you."

I near pleaded,

"What about your TV?"

She gave a nasty chuckle, said,

"I don't watch television."

Outside, I stood to take a breath.

Jericho was leaning against the car, a lollipop in her mouth.

She was the essence of smugness wrapped in a sneer.

She offered the pop, asked,

"Wanna suck?"

I asked,

"You abandon your mates, leave them to rot in jail, shoot a barman, now are planning to get rid of the old lady who has been kind to you."

I paused.

Then in a kind of desperation, asked,

"*Who are you?*"

She gave a wide smile, said,

"But you know who. I'm a Galway girl."

The younger Thomas Kroon leaned forward on the
Client's desk
And said,
"There's no real polite way to say this.
Mr. Drayton, someone's fucking our corpses
And we'd like it to stop."

Sam Wiebe, Last of the Independents

Come the end of June and a third heat wave on the way.

In Galway.

They were forecasting a shortage of CO_2 (no, me neither).

Which is what puts the kick, fizz, varoom in beer, soft drinks.

Ireland without beer, in a heat wave.

In line with this madness, the World Cup kicked off in Russia with the Spanish manager being fired twenty-four hours before kickoff.

Ronaldo scored a goal of such beauty for Portugal and we watched with wonder. It brought his European tally to eighty-five.

Messi missed a penalty that allowed Australia to look creditable.

Iceland nearly beat the hot favorite, France, which sent that little country into wild jubilation.

And Trump

Caused chaos with the policy of taking children from their immigrant parents and placing them in separate camps. World-wide condemnation had him reverse the policy but the photos of the distraught children would haunt for a long time.

Melania visited the camps with a jacket that had the large white message:

   I

      Really

         Don't care.

            Do you?

Back home Drumm, the architect of the seven billion frauds for AIB, had been hiding out in the U.S., then served five months in high-security jail there and that seems to have prompted him to risk his chances with the Irish legal system.

I mean, how bad could it be?

This asshole was on tape pouring scorn on people, wishing he could punch the finance minister in the face and making other taunts that epitomized his contempt for the people who would lose everything.

On the day Drumm was to be sentenced the press spent hours attempting to see the title of the book he was buried in.

It turned out to be a book about war journalists.

Go figure.

He was sentenced to six years.

Plenty of time to finish that book.

Much speculation, too, on what Trump and the North Korean leader had for lunch the day of their historic meeting.

Popcorn and ice cream.

I was grabbing some sun on Eyre Square when a man approached, gave me a long look, then put out his hand, said,

"I'm Gerry Dunne. Could I talk to you?"

He was mid-thirties, wearing chinos, crisp white shirt, moccasins, no socks, shades perched in his wavy black hair, the new Irish cool generation.

His face was tanned and in a certain light he might pass for good looking save for the air of seriousness that hovered round him, like a priest in civvies.

He checked,

"You are Jack Taylor?"

"I am."

He had an English accent and it sounded like Manchester, like Oasis tone. I asked,

"What's your problem?"

"My wife, she's missing."

Before I could form some sort of reply, he said,

"See, thing is, it was kind of a whirlwind gig."

More and more like Oasis.

He continued,

"I was in a club in Manchester and this girl, she asked me to dance."

Sense of wonderment in his voice.

Added,

"It was like fate, the Ed Sheeran song was playing."

Even I could guess at that one, hazarded,

"Perfect?"

He looked vaguely annoyed as if I wasn't keeping up, snapped,

"'Galway Girl.'"

And the alarm began to ring in my head. He said,

"I'm not an impulsive guy but, phew, we were married within six months."

Then head down, shamed, he said,

"She skipped town with our—well, really my—entire savings."

He produced an envelope, said,

"These are her details."

I asked,

"What's her name?"

"Jericho."

Took me a moment to digest this, then I asked,

"When you decided to hire an investigator, how long were you figuring it would take to find your wife, or how long were you prepared to pay for the time looking for her?"

He scratched his head, said,

"Depends on the daily rate."

Cute.

I said,

"Your rock-bottom guy, the very cheapest dude, would run to at least two hundred a day, plus he'd run you for expenses. So, again, how long could you afford to pay?"

He was torn: he didn't want to look like a cheap fuck but, on the other hand, how reckless was he prepared to be? He tried,

"Two weeks?"

I took out my notebook, wrote in it. He guessed I was doing the math. He guessed wrong. I said,

"Found her."

He was as close to speechless as it gets, then,

"How?"
I said,
"This is her address."
I stood, began to move off, he said,
"I don't know what to say."
I said,
"*Thanks* never hurts."

"That's what an execution is like. It's what I wit-
    nessed thirty-five years ago, what I remember of
    every sight, and sound and smell.
I'm not against the death penalty but anyone who
    ever suggests I get a morbid thrill from it—
Fuck you."

Becky Masterman, A Twist of the Knife

I got back to my apartment a few days later, knew instantly someone was there, moved cautiously inside, expecting just about anything.

Got . . .

Jericho.

Sitting in my armchair, the bottle of Jameson at her elbow, dressed in shorts, tight silk T-shirt, flip-flops, she asked,

"Wanna blow job?"

The heat wave was in its second week and already the government was warning of water shortages. I opened all the windows, trying for any trace of wind. As if reading my mind, she asked,

"Hoping for an ill wind?"

I looked at her, said,

"I think you pretty much cover that."

She laughed, raised the bottle, asked,

"Join me?"

I asked,

"Who'd you kill today?"

She stood, did a yoga stretch, letting me see the curves of her, smiled, said,

"I want to call a truce."

I laughed, a long way from feeling a trace of humor, asked,

"Oh, like, if you don't kill Jess, I forget about you?"

She nodded, said,

"That work for you?"

"No."

She pulled a mock petulant face, said,

"You're getting the better deal. I mean, you did kill my sis."

I said,

"I don't know you, how the hell would I know your sister?"

She looked like she might knife me, then,

"My sister was Emerald, who you killed. We were sisters in blood."

I said,

"And in madness, it seems."

She ignored that, said,

"I was a total wreck when she found me, strung out on crystal, no hope, and she saved me. She made me promise if anything happened to her, I was to go after you, *you,* who she worshipped, removed all the bad shit in your life."

There's very little point in arguing with your out-and-out crazy, save a bullet in the head. I asked,

"That's your grand design, kill me?"

A sly malignant smile. She said,

"But you have to suffer first."

I said,

"You're overlooking one tiny detail."

"Yeah?"

"I'll deal with you first."

She sneered,

"You're not in my class."

I opened the door, waved her out, said,

"Funny, Emerald thought the same thing."

She was halfway down the corridor when I said,

"Gerry is looking for you."

Stopped her. She asked,

"Who?"

"Your husband, Gerry Dunne."

She gave a nasty laugh, said,

"Oh. He found me, gave him a quick blow job, he gave me *the loan* of six hundred euros but, odd thing is, he decided to go swimming."

Paused, then,

"Must be the heat but Gerry . . . he never could swim."

I stared at her, then her face lit up as if a brilliant thought had occurred to her. She asked,

"Maybe I could hire you, Jack, you being a *PI*"—the sneer she managed to inject here was nearly admirable—"Do you think you could find him? Oh, that would be such a relief. I'm, like, so worried I could, you know, like scream."

She was still laughing as she skipped away.

The tape of Scott I had recorded was finally acted on by the Guards.

Jericho was arrested.

I let out a sigh of relief, thought,

"That's the end of that madness."

If only.

Her husband caught up with me in Garavan's as I was working on my first pint. I might have felt relief that she hadn't in fact drowned him but he was becoming more than a nuisance.

I wasn't expecting gratitude that my information had helped him find her but perhaps I expected a certain amount of relief.

Nope.

"You asshole,"

He launched.

Nope, not gratitude.

I gave him the slow look, asked,

"Who are you again?"

Threw him, but he rallied.

"Gerry Dunne. I hired you to find my wife."

I ordered another pint, asked him,

"You found her?"

Tentatively,

"Well, yeah."

"Did I charge you?"

"No."

I said,

"Word of advice, don't go swimming."

He was baffled, said,

"So what else?"

I let out a breath, said,

"So fuck off."

Later, a few pints to the worse, I left the pub, and waiting outside was

Gerry Dunne.

I muttered,

"Aw, for fuck's sake."

He kneed me in the balls.

Very few levels of actual agony reach the height of that pain; it soars straight to your brain as it roars.

"This is going to hurt like almighty."

It does.

Luckily, he then kicked me in the face.

I say *luckily* as it momentarily distracts your brain, which wonders,

"What fresh hell is this?"

Then they join forces to form a symphony of such utter white heat that nothing else matters save the scalding universe of hurt.

He bent down, said,

"Your nose is broken. Now I'm going to blind you."

He was grabbed from behind by someone who effortlessly tossed him across the street, then helped me to a kneeling position; standing was so out of the question. I could hear Dunne wailing,

"He had the love of my life arrested."

My helper was Sheridan, who said,

"The broken nose will give you some hint of character."

I managed to whimper,

"Just what I needed, some character."

The doctor who examined me, said,

"It's broken."

I looked at him, said,

"Wow, you're good. I'd never have known if you hadn't examined me."

He looked at my mutilated fingers, my discreet hearing aid, said,

"You've lived a rather . . ."

Searched for a description, got

"Full life."

No argument.

He said,

"You need rest. I will prescribe some painkillers for your nose and, um, various ailments."

He peered at the chart doctors seem to have attached to them, said,

"No drinking."

I prepared to leave and he stood in front of me, said,

"I'm serious, Mr. Taylor, no alcohol."

I gave him a lopsided smile. It hurt my nose. I said,

"As if."

None of them knows
How then shall we lure her back?
From the way, she goes.
  Francis Thompson, "July Fugitive"

The mail next day delivered this:

The Mayor of Galway

      And the councillors of the city

      Cordially invite you to

      The Annual Mayor's Ball

      To be held in City Hall

      On Friday, July 6th.

      Black tie

      RSVP

I tried to digest this then muttered the only thing you could.
I muttered,

    F

       U

          C

          K

            ME.

I was outside my apartment, still sweltering in the nigh
monthlong heat wave.

A black BMW was parked before me.

Gerry Dunne appeared beside it, held up a bunch of keys,
then, with slow deliberation, made a long deep gash alongside
the car, gouged in deep, stepped back, sneered,

"What do you say to that, shithead?"

I said,

"I don't have a car."

A very large man came rushing down the street, screamed, "Who the fuck did that?"

I nodded at Gerry, still brandishing the keys.

I strolled away to the sound of a severe beating and I couldn't swear to it but it did seem as if Gerry might actually be eating said keys.

I had bought the paper in Holland's, with the English team on the front pages. They beat Sweden to get a place in the World Cup semis, to face Croatia.

Their captain, with the solid name of Kane, was the new English hero.

He scored six goals in the tournament.

A pub in Connemara claimed a connection to his ancestors and the landlady promised a pint free to her customers for every goal he scored.

To her relief, he didn't score in the quarterfinal, but one Seamas Kane, who admitted to never having heard of the guy, now declared,

"He's my first cousin."

Of course he is.

Fourteen young children were trapped in a cave in Thailand for two weeks despite numerous rescue attempts. Finally, on the ninth of July, five were rescued.

A Thai navy diver lost his life as he tried to bring oxygen to the trapped group through the narrow passage, full of water.

Trump declared war on Harley-Davidson, over export taxes.

I was outside Supermac's, contemplating a bacon burger, when a black BMW pulled up before me. For a moment I thought it was the keyed car but it was mark free. The window rolled down, a young priest in the driver's seat.

And I mean young.

More altar boy than full-blown cleric and yet he had that air of a wannabe FBI.

Right down to the earpiece. He said,

"Please get in the car, Mr. Taylor."

I said,

"No."

That confused him and he was absolutely still for a moment, then,

"You will be well recompensed."

Mmm.

I asked,

"Will that be in the form of a blessing or something more tangible, because I have to say I'm all done with blessings, in disguise or indeed any form."

A trace of a smile.

It seemed to almost hurt his face, so alien was it to him.

He confirmed,

"Financial."

I got into the back, said,

"Let's bounce, time is money."

As I lay back in the car I thought of the shock, awe, of a TV program I'd watched the night before.

Atlanta.

Brainchild of Donald Glover, it was in its second series and so wickedly off-kilter you just went with the flow.

I'd just finished episode five, "Barbershop," which in essence was about an almost haircut, droll but nothing too wild, so I went into episode six, "Teddy Perkins," cold, as in knowing absolutely nothing about it.

Phew.

Blew me to hell and gone.

A forty-five-minute genius horror movie with nods to

Get Out

What Ever Happened to Baby Jane?

Michael Jackson

Child abuse

And an air of menace from the *off* that kept you completely off balance.

Creativity at its finest.

When I learned who played Teddy, I was, if possible, even more impressed.

Nice to know that the arts can still totally fuck with your head.

The car pulled up in Taylor's Hill, outside a mini mansion.

The driver explained,

"It's the residence for the bishop-in-waiting."

Malachy.

I decided to fuck a bit with the guy, asked,

"And will he be, like, waiting long?"

He took me seriously but, then, I imagined he took most things thus, said,

"We expect the announcement during His Holiness's visit."

The pope.

Who was going to cover the country in twenty-four hours, then leg it, much like Harry and Meghan's visit. These whizzing day visits were all the rage.

Expensive too.

Forty million for the pope.

I asked,

"What is your gig?"

"Excuse me?"

He let a whine into that.

I said,

"It's not a difficult question. Are you

Driver? Messenger?

Hatchet man?

Arm candy?

He had to bite down his anger, said,

"His preeminence is waiting."

I got out, said,

"So, so fuck off, then."

I was greeted at the front door by a housekeeper who seemed familiar but not in a good way.

One of those women who seem to have been born fifty, bitter, and vicious.

She snarled,

"You."

I mustered my best fake pleasant tone, said,

"Terribly sorry, I've forgotten your name."

"I remember you, Taylor, you're nothing but trouble."

Thing is, I mostly agreed with her, said,

"The good father is, I believe, expecting me."

See, nice note of piety and servitude.

She moved aside to let me in, said,

"More's the Irish pity."

Added,

"Wipe your feet."

Malachy came at me almost in a gallop.

I thought he was going to assault me but, worse, a hug.

He gushed,

"You hero, Jack."

He was dressed in white sweatpants, jet black T-shirt with the logo

V.A.T.I.C.A.N.

Into my head came the words of Tammy Wynette's

"D.I.V.O.R.C.E."

You could do a lot with the alteration of Tammy's lyrics:

. . . the V.A.T.I.C.A.N.

Took my child away.

Releasing me from the hug, he said,

"You are a wonder. I asked you to solve the problem of the girl leeching off my sister and what did you do?"

In truth, not a whole lot, but he near shouted,

"You had her arrested. Just genius."

I tried to look suitably modest but that usually translates as slightly deranged. Malachy reached behind him, grabbed an envelope, a thick one, handed it over, said,

"You'll find we've been more than generous."

Would it be, as I once heard on BBC4, *churlish* to count it?

Fuck, I can do *churlish*.

It was a lot.

Malachy continued to beam at me and, in truth, it was getting a tiny bit creepy.

A priest smiles that much at you, run.

Malachy asked,

"Did you get your invitation?"

"What?"

His delight was now edged with a wee touch of impatience. He snapped,

"To the mayor's gala."

"Uh-huh."

Took him a minute, then he emitted a mocking laugh.

"Sweet Lord, you thought you were invited."

Paused,

Searching for the most ludicrous term he could land on, took

"On your own, what? Merit?"

I thought it was only in books that people *rocked with laughter*.

Malachy rocked with laughter.

I took a deep breath, asked,

"What's the deal?"

He was still suffused with delight, said,

"You'll be my sister's escort. We have a tux ordered for you and a car will pick you up. Your job is to try to look dignified but stay fucking silent and sober."

I asked,

"What's not to love?"

"Whether it's true or not, who cares?
The truth is for teenagers and hippies.
We're too old and ugly for that crap.
Wake me up, make me think, or buy me a drink.
Otherwise, fuck off."

Michael Rutger, *The Anomaly*

The heat wave subsided.

An old woman had said,

"If there is a *yes* to the abortion referendum, Ireland will be visited by a tsunami of grief."

Is a forty-degree heat wave in that category?

I was sitting on Eyre Square, soaking up the remnants of the sunshine. The grass was scorched dark brown and little did I know a tiny tsunami was within a few yards of me.

I noticed a young woman—in her early twenties I'd guess but she was dressed like a woman caught in a fifties warp—wearing a tweed two-piece suit, like you might have glimpsed on *Mad Men*.

Her face could have been pretty save for a slight twist to her features that suggested she was elsewhere.

She approached me, said,

"Mr. Jack Taylor."

As if she were presenting me.

She immediately gave me a very uneasy feeling.

I nodded, asked,

"Was there something?"

She asked,

"May I sit down?"

Produced a dainty handkerchief (people use them anymore?), wiped the seat, then very delicately eased herself down, said,

"I'm Alice."

Then she gave a nervous laugh, added,

"My mum said,

'Alice doesn't live here anymore.'"

I thought,

"Bitch."

She had a bag, more satchel really, that, like the hankies, you never see, opened it, and threw back the flap, said,

"See, Jack, I have all your requirements."

So okay, I looked.

I saw,

Bottle of Jameson

Zippo

Pack of Camels

Shot glass

Packet of Rich tea.

Rich tea?

She giggled, said,

"The biccies are for me."

I took a deep breath, said,

"Very impressive but what do you want?"

She gave a heartaching smile, said,

"Why, Jack, I want you to find me."

The very air seemed to hold a pause in time.

I wondered if there was a neon sign above my head that proclaimed,

"All ye crazies

Lunatics

Dispossessed

Neurotics

Gather here."

I decided to momentarily swim in the insanity, asked,

"Where would I look for you?"

She said,

"I have a room with sheltered accommodation."

I said,

"That's great, Alison."

Her face became a riot of anger. She screamed,

"Alison? Are you fucking kidding me? My name is Alice! How hard is it to just remember my name? I mean what kind of detective are you going to be if the basics are beyond you."

Okay.

I stood, said,

"I'll let you know if I find you."

I heard her shout that I had forgotten the satchel.

I muttered,

"Find a gift horse to throw it on."

The mayor's ball.

A resounding success . . .

Not.

Began in a semi-okay mode. The car collected me and we managed to pick up Jess without too much drama.

Insofar as she barked at the driver to

"Get the goddamn door for me."

She was wearing a gold dress that was way too small, so all the bits of her you might not wish to see gushed forth, plus she'd had a bath in some perfume that had you instantly open all the windows.

I handed her a single red rose.

Nice move, I thought.

She snarled,

"One fucking flower. You couldn't rise to a bunch?"

I bit down, hard.

She examined my tux and, in truth, it was not a perfect fit, like one of those scarecrows that have been neglected. She asked,

"You rent that?"

I told the truth, said,

"The Church provided it."

She scoffed,

"A freaking charity case, this is who I have as an escort."

She leaned over, tapped the driver, not gently, barked,

"This might be a good time to break out the liquid refreshments."

Turned to me, said,

"When they pick me up for my role in the new *Dynasty* the limo has a wet bar."

The driver, not missing a beat, handed back a flask. I took it, uncapped it, used the top as a cup, poured freely, and handed it to her.

She smelled it, muttered,

"Cheap shite."

Drained it.

She glared at me, demanded,

"Tell me one interesting thing about you."

Sneer leaked all over her tone. I said,

"I went to jail for the murder of the mayor's son."

The driver almost crashed.

Admiration colored her face. She looked as if she might embrace me.

Shudder at the thought.

The driver, to maybe lighten the tone, asked her,

"Might I have seen you in anything?"

She sighed, turned to him, said,

"Google me."

Managed to inject it with unsettling suggestiveness.

Back to me, she asked,

"You, *you* ever see me in anything?"

I said,

"Yes."

Absolute delight, and,

"Pray tell."

"When the psycho was staying at your house?"

"Yes?"

"I saw you in jeopardy."

* * *

The ball was packed, the mighty and the wannabes.

The mayor ignored me but was all over Jess.

I found a relatively quiet corner and mostly was mistaken for the help.

Fairly surly help, in truth.

I vaguely heard introductions as the egos clashed with the alcohol.

One intro registered, a woman who was name checked as being "responsible for sheltered accommodation."

She was in her fifties, face well flushed from champagne.

I headed toward her with two drinks, handed her one, she asked, "You are?"

"An admirer."

Sufficient.

And she was sufficiently drunk that she wouldn't hit my queries with the new Irish "get out of jail free card."

Data protection.

No matter whom you asked.

Where,

Why.

The catchall reply was DP.

A classic case of bolt the door when the horse had galloped into oblivion.

The banks, health gang, gov, all let info leak like a screaming wind, then shut down when things got hot and produced this new blank answer.

I decided to try a tactic I was in short supply of:

Charm.

I sleazed,

"Your husband must be crazy to leave you alone."

Fuck.

She tittered, a horrible sound, said,

"I don't have a *hubband*."

We both laughed at the attempt to pronounce the word. What's a slurred word when you're having a bit of a time?

Now for the hook. I said,

"Alice sings your praises."

She peered at me, asked,

"Alice Bennet?"

I sure hope so, pushed,

"Just awful what happened to the poor girl."

She bit.

Said,

"That animal that attacked her, he got off scot-free."

I waited.

She was into it, continued,

"Sean Garret, his family's money kept him out of jail."

Jess came flouncing up and I do mean *flounce,* as if she were fifteen, at her first hop, and I'm not even going to mention the giggling.

She said,

"Your services are no longer required. A member of the Rotary Club will be escorting me further."

I looked at her, asked,
"As in further afield?"
She looked at me, then at the woman, sneered,
"You can have him."
The woman, actually gasping, asked,
"Was that Fionnula Flanagan?"
I nodded,
She shook her head, said,
"What a bitch."

As you left the ball there was a table with the Irish version of
the goodies bag, said to contain
A signed photo of the mayor,
A sliothar (the ball used in hurling),
And a free pass to the plowing championships.
I lined up for my *mala,* Irish for bag, and was refused.
I asked,
"Why not?"
The answer,
"Only for the significant invited."
I slouched out to the car, was about to climb into the front,
when the driver said,
"No can do, Jack."
Aw, for fuck's sake.
I said,

"'Tis the night that keeps on giving."

I gave the tux jacket to a homeless guy, who used it as a bed for his dog, said,

"Didn't suit you anyway."

Quite.

Galway

Girls

Gomorrah

It would be the summer of the Galway girls.

Summer of dead girls.

The Galway Races began and the rain returned
With a vengeance.
I was summoned by Malachy.
I don't really do *summoned*.
The same young priest from before at my door.
I had a ferocious hangover.
One of those, *I'll kill someone*.
I snarled,
"You have a name?"
He caught the tone, said meekly,
"Pat."
I threw open the door, said,
"I need a coffee, probably the hair of the dog."
He ventured in slowly as I began to make the coffee. He dared,
"Um, I'm not sure we have time for that."
I didn't even look at him, said,
"Sit the fuck down, shut up, and don't speak until I'm on
the other side of two coffees, three cigs, and anything else I can
keep in my gut."
I poured two mugs of coffee, thought about it, then added a
slug of Jay to both.

KEN BRUEN

The mugs, wittily enough, proclaimed:

Mug 1

Mug 2

Cute.

The first cig nigh killed me and Pat tried,

"Is that a good idea?"

I laughed.

"Good idea? Jesus, I haven't had one of those since 1957."

He drank the coffee and I could see his color rise, the Jay almost instant in its effect.

He looked at his watch, said,

"He won't be best pleased."

I waited a beat, then,

"Fuck him."

And he laughed.

I grabbed his mug, said,

"Lemme top that up."

Added a fair dollop of Jay, handed him the mug, he took it willingly.

I let him get on the other side of that, then,

"What's his big hurry?"

He was lit up, said,

"He is mighty pissed."

. . . *bit like yourself,*

I thought.

He was all chat now, said,

"Jericho got bail."

Fuck.

He added,

"Jess put up her home as bond."

Not good.

I sent Pat away, muttering I had to get on this right away.

Pat crashed the car one street away.

Oops.

Sean Garret, the rapist

Who'd destroyed the young woman Alice's life?

Alice, who wanted me to find *her*.

Figured, first I'd find Garret.

Google showed him to be

"One of our future leaders."

Not if I found him.

Photos of him were extremely flattering.

Good looking in a slightly going-to-seed fashion, shaggy blond hair, almost surfer dude but with Armani suits.

His family owned one of the major construction companies and, at twenty-two, he was already a director, owned a Porsche, had a girlfriend who'd been on one of those *Love Island* shows.

Like all the new Irish who had Hollywood teeth and the awareness of a hedge fund.

The new generation, who didn't have any talent but had burning ambitions:

To be *seen*
To be *worshipped*
To be *envied.*
Twitter, Instagram, Snapchat, the new shrines.
For all the glitter, shininess, they exuded a deadly dullness.

I went to Charlie Byrne's. It had been a time since I saw Vinny.

He was behind the counter, chatting to Noirin, a stalwart of the bookshop.

Vinny said,

"You're looking well, Jack."

We all took a moment to savor this nice, if blatant, lie.

Noirin said,

"We hear you're keeping company with a famous actress."

Jess.

And *keeping company*

Has a myriad of meanings, from the sublime to the banal.

I said,

"She's the reason I'm here."

Vinny gave that knowing smile, ventured,

"You're going to bring her up to speed on crime fiction?"

Close.

I said,

"She's up for the leading part in the BBC adaptation of *Country Diary of an Edwardian Lady.*"

Noirin said,

"We do have a copy of that with all the original drawings, poems in her own hand, but it's dear."

I.e., expensive.

Vinny said,

"Oh, I'm sure we can help with that."

It was indeed a beautiful volume, reason why Kindle could never hope to dominate the market.

Noirin wrapped it in the bookshop's distinctive bag, said,

"You'll be well in now."

You'd think after my more than fractured relationship with Jess the last thing I'd do was buy her a gift.

She was indeed full of bluster and bullshit.

But

Somewhere in that entire complicated front I had glimpsed a frightened child.

I kind of admired her blunt embrace of life, to face all with a shot of gin and cheek. She was that rarity: an original and a ferocious pain in the arse.

I got home and instantly knew someone had been there.

I moved cautiously around and, in the bedroom, hanging from the light was a black noose.

Black as in jet-black rope.

On the bed was a sheet of black notepaper with red lettering that read,

"*Hang loose.*"

* * *

A body was hanging from the Spanish Arch.

A crowd gathered quickly and word spread that it was the actress from *Dynasty*.

One guy ventured,

"Christ, now that's a bad review."

The Guards arrived and it took hours to process the scene and finally take the body down.

The American who'd discovered the body later said to his wife,

"Remember our first night here?"

She did, said,

"Sure, hon, we went to see *Playboy of the Western World.*"

He nodded soberly, then,

"The dress the body was in, it was the same as Peg."

She asked,

"You think they hung her after the performance?"

He loved his wife but, Jesus H, sometimes . . .

The Guards didn't have to appeal for witnesses.

If anything, they had too many.

The square in front of the arch is party central in the summer.

Beside the square is one of the ugliest buildings in the city, a gray slab of

Concrete, known as *The Kremlin.*

The tenants were tormented every night by

Bongos

Girls screeching
Fights
And, inevitably,
A horrendous version of "The Fields of Athenry."
You couldn't give the bloody apartments away.

Picture this:

A long-framed shot, the camera ready to zoom in.

An American, on his first visit to Ireland, name of Danny Rourke, is standing on the steps of Jurys hotel, bottom of Quay Street.

It's just past dawn and Danny, all the way from St. Paul, Minnesota, has sneaked out to smoke a cig. He hadn't smoked for thirty years but, hey, it's his vacation and it's Galway.

Go party.

He lights the cig with a Zippo he bought from Brendan Holland, the newsagent on Eyre Square. It has a Claddagh ring on the side.

He loves that.

He stares at the Spanish Arch, about five hundred yards away, through a light mist.

Soft Irish rain.

Yes,

He mutters,

"Jumping Jehovah."

A body is hanging from a rope, swinging in the breeze of the arch.

He had only recently retired from the St. Paul Fire Department and his training kicked in. He dropped the cig, ran toward the sight.

Maybe it was a prop from the Arts Festival; all sorts of weird shit were posed around the city.

He reached the figure and let out a soft

. . . *fuck.*

It was an elderly woman dressed in some sort of costume with a placard around her neck.

It read,

> *Play*
>
> *Dead.*

No, the Guards were not short of witnesses.

One guy had spoken to two girls in white overalls and Arts Festival T-shirts who were bringing a mannequin to the top of the arch.

He and his buddy helped them with the ladders!

The young ladies were extremely grateful.

The ban Garda who was interviewing them as her sergeant supervised asked,

"Can you give me a description?"

Guy One said,

"Big ladders."

The sergeant had to suppress a guffaw.

The ban Garda tried,

"The girls, what were they like?"

As one, the guys chorused in quasi-American,

"*Smokin'*."

In disbelief, the Garda asked,

"They were smoking?"

The sergeant bit his lip to keep the smirk away as Guy Two said,

"Hot, like, you know, smokin' hot."

The ban Garda wanted to chuck her notebook in the water—and the guys, too.

One of the guys said as she turned away,

"Lemme write this in your notebook."

A clue?

She handed over a loose page and the guy, laboring, gouged out numbers. Young people don't actually, like, *write*.

They text.

Hence his apparent difficulty.

He handed the paper back.

She stared at it, near dizzy with hope, asked,

"You got their number?"

He fizzled with annoyance, said,

"That's my number."

She snapped the notebook shut, began to stride away.

Her sergeant said,

"You have the perfect blend of persistence and stupidity, you'll go far."

Then added,

"Now if you only played hurling."

They spoke to a range of other witnesses and got little more.

As they headed toward Jurys for a tea break, one of the guys shouted,

"Call me."

The funeral of an actress
Is drama.
The funeral of an actress /
Galway girl
Is melodrama.

Headline in the papers:

Actress

     in

         Suicide/Murder

            Mystery

Fuck, the papers went wild with the death of Jess.

Speculation as to whether her über-loyal fans had helped her stage a grand exit,

Or if they'd killed her.

The obvious suspect was Jericho.

But

She'd a solid alibi.

The air of mystery/mystique in Jess's death was fueled, too, by the now heavily publicized fact that she was—

Shock, horror, delight—

The bishop's sister.

That he wasn't yet bishop didn't matter.

The lurid ingredients were there:

The bishop,

The actress,

A lesbian?

And

Siblings.

More than enough to sell a ton of papers.

And they sold.

Malachy sent me a short terse text:

This is your fault,

You bollix.

Now, if I showed that to the papers, I could have named my price.

The

      Bishop

           and

                the

                    Bollix

(They could have added this headline.)

The American who'd first spotted the body became a minor celebrity

And enjoyed it.

Sure beat fighting fires.

The *Galway Advertiser* had this:

"Exclusive with Danny Rourke"

By Kernan Andrews.

Jimmy Norman on his hugely popular radio show had him as his guest.

Jimmy asked,

"So, Danny, your initial impression on seeing the body hanging underneath the arch?"

Danny had developed a deeper voice since his brush with fame, felt gravitas was necessary, and also made sure to wait a few beats before answering.

This implied:

Solemnity

Sorrow

Thoughtfulness

Or he was just a thick fuck.

He said,

"James"—always use the interviewer's name, a lot—"I thought first it was like a prank."

His tone rising at the end to suggest a question.

Jimmy didn't know.

Which is why he was asking him, but he nodded carefully, which is always dicey on radio but Jimmy had been at this game a while.

Danny, getting into it, said,

"Me and the missus"—he spoke thus as he was told it impressed the ordinary listener—"we'd been to the Druid . . ."

Paused.

"Like, you know, the Druid, the theater?"

As if.

Jimmy sighed, said patiently,

"We are familiar with our world-famous theater."

Sarcasm alas is lost on visiting Americans as they still believe, despite all evidence to the contrary, that we are well-wishing folk.

Rourke, taking this as encouragement, if not exactly as approval, warmed to his narrative.

Like this:

"So Deb and I . . ."

Pause.

"She's my better half. We had been to see *Playboy of the Western World*."

Jimmy interrupted fast lest Rourke explain that play.

"We know it."

Rourke, thrown a wee bit, wondering did he detect a hint of impatience?

Faltered, then cautiously proceeded.

"Peg's costume was remarked on many times by Deb and when I saw the, um,

Body, Jesus H, it was the same outfit."

Caught himself, corrected this,

"Well, not the exact one, of course, but, buddy, it was a ringer."

Jimmy looked up to see Keith Finnegan making the

Wrap it up!

Signal.

Said to Rourke,

"Thank you for coming in, and safe travel."

Rourke stood, slightly flummoxed, asked,

"Can you validate parking?"

* * *

Michael Whelan had been a classmate of mine, back when corporal punishment was a daily reality.

Patrician Brothers were the outfit/teachers.

Semireligious in that, as they weren't priests, they simmered with massive chips on their collective dandruffy cassocks.

I went on to become a failure in many fields while Michael came first in college in chemistry, no mean feat.

He was the envy of all the kids on our street as he owned a red rocket.

Not the Branson mode but a toy that you actually lit and it fired into the sky and our wistful imaginations.

He was the first person I ran into at the funeral of Jess.

Her blend of

Fame

Infamy

Notoriety

Suicide/murder

Ensured a mega-attendance

From the great, the glorious Galwegians.

Michael said,

"She has drawn a bigger crowd than St. Thérèse will."

The remains of the saint were due to be processioned through the streets in a few days.

You outdraw a saint in Galway, you're really something.

I said,

"She was really something."

I think he thought I meant the saint.

Pat, the young priest who walked point for Malachy, came rushing over.

"Nice,"

I thought.

"He's going to welcome me."

If *welcome* is the apt term for a funeral.

He was red in the face, glared at Michael Whelan, then almost shouted at me,

"You're barred."

I gasped,

"From a funeral?"

He did look a little ashamed but not much, said,

"His preeminence says he'll call the Guards."

I have been barred from the best

Pubs

Clubs

Weddings

Rotary club

Legion of Mary.

But this . . .

A new low in a life slowly but with indefinite purpose crawling toward the pit.

Worse, I had the book I bought for Jess in my Garda jacket.

In some mad romantic notion, I'd seen my own self gently toss the book in after the coffin.

I offered the book to Pat, asked,

"Will you hand this to Malachy, with my deepest sympathy?"

He stared with utter scorn at me, said,

"In words his preem might use . . ."

Pause . . .

"Shove it up your arse."

                    So,

What to do with a book you can't literally bury.

Give it to a nun.

Sister Maeve. Had been too long since I saw her.

The American term *regifting* was pretty much my intention and I have to say it's a *neat* notion.

You take your *un*wanted gift / no longer a use for gift, etc. Pass it on.

A. You get rid of the bloody thing.

B. You get gratitude for it.

Pretty much

                Win

                Win

Or so I believed.

She was delighted to see me, gave me a megahug and, trust me, you get a hug from a nun it's unlike any other hug,

Ever.

She looked, as always, in her late thirties and I knew her to be nunning toward mid-fifties.

I have used this term before as it kind of belongs in *Lives of the Saints.*

She had a beatific smile.

Made you feel better than you were or you'd ever be.

Being hugged by a nun is, oddly, both sacred and profane.

Ushered me into the small apartment she used as outrider for the Poor Clares.

I said,

"I brought you a gift, you know, to . . ."

(Lie, quick.)

"Celebrate the pope's visit."

The pope's visit had the country in a tizzy.

Forty million it was to cost.

Mind you, various sources quoted forty million or at least thirty million, but either way a lot.

Papal merchandise was hot.

In Lidl you could buy lolli-popes.

So, in the U.S., would there be pope-cicles?

The pope's face was on the front of the lollipop but if you sucked all the way it didn't sustain; his image evaporated.

I know, there is a blasphemous joke in there somewhere but I'm not seeking it.

The pope would be in the country for twenty-four hours, culminating in Mass at Croke Park.

Now here's where it gets weird:

Temporary morgues were being arranged as so many pilgrims were expected but—

Big but—

Due to security, snipers on rooftops (I shit thee not), no vehicles were allowed within a ten-mile radius.

Ten!

So elderly folks, along with the other poor bastards, had to walk ten miles just to reach the venue. They might just get there to hear Nathan Carter sing.

More contention:

The most popular priest in the whole country was Father Ray Kelly, whose impromptu singing of "Hallelujah" at a wedding, to the delight and amazement of the congregation and a swooning bride, went viral, over two million hits on YouTube. He appeared on *England's Got Talent* with a version of "Everybody Hurts."

That shook you to your very hurt soul.

He was doing nigh the impossible—restoring people's faith in a priest.

Would they let him sing for the pope?

Like fuck.

Let's have the mediocre Carter,

Who mainly tortured "Proud Mary."

A PR flunkey hired by the Church told the pilgrims to

Train

Plan

Get fit,

As if to climb Croagh Patrick.

It's our mini-Everest, with religious bonus points, spiritual air miles in a fashion.

Forty or so million for the dignitaries but no buses for the faithful.

Maeve's apartment was Zen, clean, fresh, and warm, and she produced a bottle of Jack Daniel's—my fault, as I'd introduced her to Jameson.

So she got the wrong stuff; sue me.

She poured two walloping measures into Galway crystal glasses and then looked oh, so sad, said,

"My father gave me these. He said they would be a great start when I met the right man and got married."

Fuck, a tiny tear escaped, rolled slowly down one wind-tanned cheek. I rushed,

"But you did."

Her head snapped up.

"Who?"

I said, as seriously as possible (this was vital),

"The man *Himself,* Our Lord."

Good heavens, I sounded like Johnny Cash.

Went with the bourbon, I guess.

She loved that.

"And I got you a gift."

She handed over a package, a very large bag. I opened it and pulled out what appeared to be a wax jacket.

She purred,

"It's Barbour. The convent was given a shipment that the stores couldn't sell."

A whole other branch of regifting?

The devil was in me, so I said,

"But I have my Garda coat."

Thick as fuck, right?

She looked crushed, said.

"But that ould coat is falling apart."

Like my own self.

Others grow old with their husbands/wives.

Me, with a Guard's coat.

She asked,

"Will you try it?"

I said,

"To tell the truth (always a precursor to a lie) I kind of associate wax jackets with the royal family and toffs massacring pheasants."

She began to laugh, said,

"You're a holy terror."

I wore the damn jacket, black it was, as my heart, but it did have a lot of pockets so there's that.

She stood back to admire it, said,

"You look like the gentry."

I said,

"I'm elected."

She then opened the gift I brought her, made a breath of admiration when she saw the cover, then opened it and read in bewilderment

. . . *to*

> *My*
>> *Favorite*
>>> *Actress*

Oh, fuck.

I tried, said,

"I mean you act like, um, life is simple."

She put the book aside with a sigh and, shortly afterward, I left in my new coat.

Outside, on the small wall, sat,

Jericho,

Who sneered,

"Fucking a nun."

I said,

"The bloody wall of Jericho."

We stared at each other for a long Galway minute, hostility dancing on the very air.

She asked,

"How much do I remind you of Emerald?"

I told the whole truth.

"You're a piss-poor copycat, you have no style, no wit, and you're almost English, killing a defenseless old woman. That's who you are."

And for the very first and only time in my life I spat.

Literally.

Continued,

"That's what I think of you."

It landed on her much-scuffed Doc Martens boot. She was dressed in faux combat gear, all too big for her, and she resembled a petulant child in her dad's clothes.

Her face went through a range of emotions.

Part shock

Rage

A hint of fear

And then the defiance.

She snarled,

"Surely you admired the street theater of the old bitch's death. Come on, Jack, it was impressive."

I asked,

"Who was the other scum helping you?"

A smile of malevolence. She said,

"An apprentice, an intern, if you will."

I felt tired and said,

"Tell her she's facing early retirement."

She clapped her hands, said,

"Oh, goody gumdrops. You're coming after us."

I began to walk away, she yelled,

"The jacket makes you look like a ponce."

I gave her the finger without breaking stride and she hollered,

"I thought you loved Galway girls."

I snapped back,

"Only the Steve Earle version, and maybe Mundy's."

Jericho remembered the day she killed her father.

She'd come home unexpectedly, bearing a bottle of Hennessy brandy,

His favorite.

He'd received her coldly,

Asked,

"What do you want?"

She purred,

"To make peace."

Before he could answer, she headed for the drinks cabinet, poured two glasses of the brandy, said,

"Drink first, and then I have some amazing news."

He drank,

She didn't.

Took maybe two minutes before he began to clutch his chest, gulp furiously.

She said,

"No hurry, it will take a few agonizing minutes before it actually kills you."

He was on his knees, she knelt, said,

"I pushed Gina into the traffic."

Then she said,

"Oh, my God, I almost forgot to tell you my news."

Hit her head with an open palm in mock reprimand, then,

"It's amazing that I didn't kill you years ago."

His body jerked in spasms, then he was still.

Jericho stared at him for a moment, then said,

"Bye-bye, Daddy."

This killing grip is an old deep pattern in her brain.
Stimulus: people.
Response: kill.
At half past six, a small, unhappy wail
Came from a baby.
Straightaway, the hawk
Drove her talons into my glove,
Ratcheting up the pressure
In savage, stabbing spasms.
Kill, the baby cries.
Kill
     Kill
       Kill.

           Helen Macdonald, *H Is for Hawk*

Galway lost the All Ireland by one point.

One damn point, which, in hurling, is like nothing.

We didn't begrudge Limerick the win so much as they'd waited forty-five years for the title and the Liam Cup still crossed the Shannon.

In Galway, Jericho pulled herself from a deep, untroubled sleep, stretched like the feline she was, then began to roll a spliff. Her lover stirred slowly, purred,

"Come back to bed, babe."

Jericho lit the spliff with the Zippo she'd stolen from Jack Taylor's apartment. She truly got off on breaking in there, leaving weird things behind—this time, a small statue of Shiva, thought,

"The dumb bollix probably thought it was a Marvel figurine."

But,

She had to admit he was showing a resilience that surprised her, knew she would have to kill him soon, but it was such a rush to mind-fuck him.

Her lover sat up, reached for the spliff as her other hand traced the tattoo etched on Jericho's back; it was of the Archangel Azrael.

"The Angel of Destruction, known as a sibling of Lucifer."

She moved in front of Jericho, her naked body as a lure.

Jericho had been fingering a chain around her neck, the tiny gold pendant with two letters,

GG.

The second *G* was almost emerald.

She slipped it off, put it round the neck of her lover, who purred, guessed,

"*GG*, is that good grief?"

Jericho was very quiet, then said,

"Galway girl."

Her lover knew not to push,

Asked,

"What's the plan today?"

Jericho smiled with utter malevolence, asked,

"How'd you like to kill a nun?"

After they had arranged a batch of very sharp knives, Jericho paused, asked,

"Is there one with a serrated blade?"

Her lover laughed, asked,

"What does it matter?"

Jericho said,

"The serrated edge makes the pain sharper."

Her lover was puzzled, so Jericho said,

"Nuns, they practice exquisite pain, it's part of their gig."

Her lover asked,

"But what's the point?"

Jericho gave a full smile, laden with witchery, said,

"Bonus points: more pain, more glory."

Her lover said,

"Sounds nuts."

Jericho sneered,

"They're nuns, they married God, and you want them to be sane as well."

The most beautiful, fastest, lethal, brutal
Killer
On the planet
Is the falcon.

What do I know about hockey?

Sweet fuck all.

But the guys in the pub were weighing the merits of the women's hockey team being in the World Cup final against Holland.

One said,

"'Tis marvelous. First time Ireland has been in a World Cup."

Silence.

Then the second fellah said,

"But women?"

A third said,

"The Dutch do nothing else but play hockey and the team is professional, our crowd are part-timers."

A fourth asked,

"What's the difference between hockey and camogie?"

Good question, I thought.

A woman said,

"Camogie is for ladies."

Echoing Queen Victoria, who said *ladies are not lesbian.*

Utter silence.

Then the bar guy said,

"Camogie is hurling for chicks."

Where this would have gone is beyond me, but then Owen Daglish came up to the counter, ordered a large Jay.

I joked,

"Bad day on the beat?"

He said,

"It is for you."

Took the glass and motioned me to a quiet corner, asked,

"How do you know a nun, Sister Maeve?"

Jesus.

I said,

"Why?"

My heart in my mouth.

He took a slug from the Jay, gulped, said,

"She was stabbed."

He had to stop, take a deep breath, then added in horror,

"Forty-eight times."

I barely managed to ask,

"Why come to me?"

He drained the glass, said,

"A book was shredded over her."

Reached for his notebook, checked, said,

"*Country Diary of an Edwardian Lady.* A page near saturated in blood had a dedication on it."

Again the notebook.

"To my favorite actress."

Signed, he said,

"Jack Taylor."

And scrawled on it, in black marker, was,

"*Act dead, bitch.*"

On the walls, in blood,

"Lucifer's sister"

Was scrawled.

I was outside the pub, puking my guts out. Owen asked,

"You all right, mate?"

Like, hello.

I asked,

"Any witnesses?"

He considered how much he could disclose, then,

"A few people saw two young women in Arts Festival T-shirts."

I thought,

"Same duo as killed Jess."

I nearly said,

"That's what happens when you cut the arts funding."

I managed to say,

". . . *sometimes with the heart,*

Seldom with the soul,

Scarcer once with flight,

Few . . . love at all."

He went,

"Wot?"

It was a poem on the wall of her home. I didn't even know I knew it, said,

"Nothing, just drink rambling."

I told the Guards everything about Jericho but, with the logistics of

The papal visit,

A huge influx of tourists,

There was not a whole lot they could do.

They figured the nun's death was by some deranged junkie.

I went to see the Mother Superior of Maeve's order.

She was stoic but I could see the deep distress etched on her face.

She said with trepidation,

"We don't assign blame, accepting God's will in all things."

But

"We do feel that your friendship with her was . . ."

Long tense silence, then,

"Culpable."

Sounded like assigning blame to me.

I asked,

"May I attend her burial?"

No fucking way.

She didn't, of course, put it that way but same song, did say,

"That would not be our wish."

Crushed, I turned to go when she relented a tad, handed me a small red rosary, said,

"To remember Our Sister with."

I knew it, had been blessed by Padre Pio as a tag on the end said, so

You don't get much holier links.

I said,

"That would not be our wish."

And got the fuck out of there, my heart in flitters.

I went to the Protestant church of St. Nicholas, my second visit there.

Dated back to 1320. Despite being not exactly a church where Catholics flock, it is held in great affection by Galwegians. Maeve once *confessed* to loving the calm of its medieval churchyard.

She had said to me,

"I'm still shocked by what happened all those years ago."

She meant hundreds of years ago, when Cromwell's army defaced it, desecrated it, and stabled their horses there.

Of all the characteristics I loved about Maeve, it was that pure naive innocence that she never lost.

Her delight in chocolate.

The wicked joy in sipping Jameson.

Her childlike delight in receiving presents.

I sat in a pew, tears coursed down my face.

I thought of desecration, her terror, her cherished rosary beads that they had strangled her with, in addition to the forty-eight stab wounds.

I could see it

                Hear it

                                Smell the blood

I howled.

Howled like a beaten dog that cannot be consoled.

I said to myself, I will wreak havoc on Jericho.

When you buy a bouquet of flowers for
A dead nun,
A Galway girl,
You leave them on the altar
In
A Protestant church.
Why?
Because you are half mad with grief.
You buy Black Bush instead of Jameson
As it's the Protestant choice.
You burn the only photo
You ever had of the beloved nun,
Then you pour the fine whiskey
Off the end of Nemo's Pier.

The pope came, and although he didn't outright admit liability for the pedophiles he did say they were *filth*.

I had one aim: find Sean Garret, the guy who destroyed the life of

Alice Bennet, the young woman who came to me and asked, "Will you find me?"

I'd sure as fuck find him.

I did.

He was the son of wealthy parents (aren't they always), a star rugby player, had the looks of a young Sean Penn, which might account for the mean streak.

I did as they do in contemporary crime fiction: I hacked his social media outlets.

Okay, I paid a young student to do it.

Garret was very active in/on

Twitter

Instagram

Snapshot

And a date app called

Gogetim.

Cute.

I followed him for a week. He did desultory attendance at the construction firm part owned by his father but played a lot of rugby and clubbed—a lot.

I finally cornered him alone one Friday evening as he strolled from his car, Ray-Bans perched on his head, white sweater tied loosely round his shoulders, a cut-rate Gatsby.

I swung my hurley and took out his right knee; there went the rugby career. He crumpled, agony on his face, screeched,

"Why?"

I was raising the hurley to smash his nose when he pleaded,

"Tell me what I did?"

I was ablaze with rage, snarled,

"Alice, remember her?"

His face changed from total agony to incredulity. He gasped,

"My ex?"

Then he stared at me, said,

"You have to be Taylor. She said she'd get you to come after me."

WTF.

A terrible comprehension was dawning in his eyes. I could see it. He held up his hand to shield himself from the hurley, said,

"I can't believe she did it. It's that fucking lesbian who put her up to it."

An insane crystallization was pulling at the edge of my mind. I took out my flask, took a wallop, offered it to him. He drank and winced.

I leaned against his car, took out cigs, lit us up.

He said,

"I shouldn't, with the training, but . . ."

Indicated his ruined leg.

Continued,

"She once told me if I ditched her she'd cry *rape*, even get into a vulnerable shelter, not that she'd spend much time there, just enough to fake out the carers. And here's the weird bit . . ."

The agony of his ruined knee kicked in on a fresh wave and he howled with the intensity of it.

I handed him the flask and he drank deep, muttered,

"Thanks."

Then continued,

"Alice had this scheme to entrap you, pretend she was fucked, and blame me, in every sense, then get you to hammer the be-jaysus out of me for ditching her."

He looked at me, said drily,

"Seems to have worked."

I tried to get my mind around the way I had been played, then asked,

"Her lesbian friend, lemme guess, is her name . . ."

I had to take a breath, then uttered,

"Jericho?"

He nodded.

I put the hurley back in my kit bag, muttered,

"Sorry, I guess."

He limped away, said,

"That really, *really* helps."

Dancing

with

Jesus

As I headed home, the kit bag slung over my shoulder, the hurley sticking out like a very bad idea,

I was a maelstrom of

Rage

Shame

Humiliation.

To be played, and so expertly.

My apartment overlooks Galway Bay. When I walk along the promenade the sight of the ocean usually makes me yearn.

I stopped, saw two young men in their twenties and, what?

Were they lighting a fire?

Fuck.

No, a makeshift spit and, to my horror, I saw a large bird struggling near their feet. They were hollering and high-fiving.

I eased down onto the sand and approached, asked,

"What's up, guys?"

Almost friendly.

The first one turned, mocked in a South Carolina accent,

"Gonna make us a little chicken dinnah."

He was on some dope that made his movements just that little bit delayed, but the second guy,

A whole other country.

Built like the proverbial brick shithouse, he was wearing a muscle shirt, shorts, and, get this, Doc Martens. He was slugging hard from a bottle of Jack Daniel's. His tone was menace in neon. He said,

"Get the fuck off, yah old cunt, or you'll join this buzzard on the spit."

The first guy was just your ordinary dumb brain-dead ejit but this number, he was a violence junkie.

I looked at the poor *buzzard*. It had what looked like a broken wing, and each time it tried to scuttle away the second guy stood on the bird and relished the rush of cruelty.

I dropped the bag, took out the hurley, asked the first guy,

"You're from Dublin?"

He nodded and got a hard shoulder from the second, who snarled,

"Don't talk to the bollix."

I said,

"The reason I ask is Sunday you guys play Tyrone in the All Ireland football final."

I swung the hurley, dropped the ejit fast.

Continued in a quiet tone,

"See, I prefer the hurling."

The dangerous one, true to form, produced a Stanley knife, blade of choice for your lower-grade thug, hissed,

"Gonna cut yer fucking bollocks off."

Lunged at me. I stepped aside and walloped his skull as he went.

That's all he sang.

I put out the fire, resisted the compulsion to put the psycho on the spit.

Took a long draft of my flask, then gently lifted the wounded bird. It did try to bite me but, then, everything does.

I could tell it was a very frightened creature, and if I had to guess there and then, I would have hazarded a hawk of some kind.

Headed back to my apartment. Apart from cooking the bird, I had very little idea what the hell I was going to do.

I said,

"If you live, I'll call you Maeve."

I did remember a line from the movie *The Great Northfield Minnesota Raid*.

A greenhorn asks a grizzled cowboy,

"What's the name of your horse?"

The cowboy spits juice, then drawls,

"Don't name something you might have to eat."

Argue that.

Got back to my apartment to find Jericho had again been *visiting*.

Left a note, of course, and a small figurine of Jesus.

The note:

> *Jack*
> *This is a dancing Jesus.*
> *There is a chorus line of the apostles doing a conga line behind him.*

Do you miss that nun? So

$$So$$

$$Bad$$

It's so sad, boo-hoo.

(Then an emoji of a crying face.)

I'll slit your throat while you sleep and then Alice will ride your
dead dick.

xxxxx

J.

I tentatively put a hand on the figurine,

And

Jesus danced.

Never
      Rely
            On who you think you are.
Never
      Rely
            On what you think you know.
Do
      Rely
            On
                Murphy's law.

*Alice came out of the shower. She'd taken a
while as it was a bitch to get blood from under your fingernails.*

Jericho was listening to Leonard Cohen.

The same track always,

"You Want It Darker."

Some interpreted the title as a question,

Others as a command.

Jericho looked up, a piece of Maeve's bloody skirt in her hands,

Asked,

"You think that's dark enough for them?"

Pa Connell is a vet and a close friend.

He'd once said to me,

"Jack, you need something, call day or night."

You say that and, though sincere, the last friggin' thing you
want is a guy calling you after midnight.

I mean, fuckit.

When I had the dogs, and it kills me to even mention them,
their passing nigh murdered me, Pa was a constant source of
help and support.

I called him now.

Woke him too.

I could hear his wife mumbling.

I begged,

"Let me see you now."

"Christ. Jack, it's two in the morning."

I didn't want to shout,

"I know the fucking time."

I whined instead.

"It's a matter of life and death."

How could he refuse?

He didn't, said,

"I'll be in my surgery in an hour."

I had the bird wrapped in a light blanket, with a makeshift hood for its eyes to fool it into sleeping.

It wasn't fooled, tried to bite me every opportunity.

I figured it was a very fine peregrine falcon—

Not only a beautiful bird but valuable,

Unless it died.

I swore,

"Don't you fucking dare die."

When Pa saw me, saw the bird, he exclaimed,

"A bird?"

I nodded.

He gently took the creature from me, laid it on his vet's table, pulled on thick gloves.

I began to ask him . . .

His hand shot up, he said,

"Don't talk,"

I didn't.

For ten minutes, he worked on the bird, having given it a shot to calm it. I could have done with some of it. Pa made sounds like

"Um, ah, I see, well, well, who knew?"

Finally, he finished, and the bird seemed to be sleeping. He said,

"It's a peregrine falcon. It has been shot by some sick bastard but this is a full-grown bird and, I'd say, rare enough in these parts. How did you get it?"

I told him.

He rummaged in a drawer, produced a bottle of brandy, poured two, asked,

"What will you do with it?"

I wanted Jameson but, in a bind, drank, said,

"I think you should keep it."

He gave a short harsh laugh, said,

"You're even madder than ever."

I was thinking I might be a wee bit offended, asked,

"What on earth would I do with a falcon?"

He said,

"There's a guy I know, not well but enough, his name is Keefer. His name is from his years as roadie for the Rolling Stones. He also moonlit, so to speak, as a film extra and, while on the movie *The Falcon and the Snowman*, in trade for Stones tickets he got to hang with the film's falconer and the rest, as they say, is, if not history, at least notable. A Scot, I think, lives out in the country, eccentric, so you should get on. He is supposedly one of the best falconers but he's very . . ."

Paused.

"Hard-core."

I had no idea what that meant so pushed,

"Will he take the bird?"

Pa got a large cage, gently laid the sleeping bird in there, said,

"I'll call him and should have an answer in a day or two. I'll keep it until then but be prepared."

"For what?"

He sighed.

"If—and that's a big if—he agrees to see you, you'd better pack for a few weeks' stay."

I was sure he was kidding, asked,

"Why on earth would I do that. He can keep the falcon, no charge, valuable bird, he should be grateful."

Pa laughed, said,

"It will take some serious training."

I said with relief,

"He can train the bird for months, good luck to them."

Pa, and I swear I saw devilment in his eyes, said,

"Not the bird, you."

Did I still even like the Stones?

Well, I could fake it,

Couldn't I?

* * *

Back at my apartment, I found an old Stones album, played it.

I had a book on rock myths, flicked through it, came across this:

"Mick Taylor is the only one to leave the Stones and live."

How encouraging was that?

Deoch

An

Doras

(The Parting Gift)

Few sayings in Irish have been interpreted in so many
different ways.
There are those who see it simply as a gift of farewell;
Others, the optimists probably, who believe it's a
blessing;
And those of us,
From the dark,
Who know it to be the ultimate curse.

As I prepared to leave my note for Jericho, I felt rage of biblical size, but after a large Jay, two Xanax, I felt sufficiently detached or, more to the point, in that part of my mind that is icy cold, a zone where nothing lives save sheer homicide.

If I was going to spend time with the eccentric falconer, I needed to put some plans in place:

1. Deal with Alice.
2. Leave a letter for Jericho for when she next housebroke.
3. Respect the passing of Maeve.
4. Buy supplies for my time away.

Finding Alice, I was supposed to be a detective of sorts, so I found her.

She was in the phone book.

Go figure.

Either stupidity or arrogance.

I watched her for six days and, on the seventh night, caught up with her as she staggered to her flat, the worse for wear drinkwise.

I said,

"Maeve sends her love."

I did what I had to do.

And

   I

      Did

         It

            With

               Slow

                  Measured

                     Deliberation.

The second week, I had Liam Garvey of the gift shop on Shop Street cut me a scroll of ogham on slate.

Ogham is one of the oldest of alphabets.

The word for love, *Gra*,

Is like a cross, with seven horizontal lines, and is read from the bottom up.

I took it to the Circle of Life Garden in Salthill.

Founded in 2014 to commemorate the organ donors whose giving has saved countless lives, it is a haven of beautiful peace. You take some water from the well that is hundreds of years old, then stroll on and reach a lake where a steel heron rises from the water.

It is staggeringly beautiful.

I placed the ogham for Maeve in the water and said a silent Hail Mary.

I said it in Irish.

It begins

Ar mhathair.

On my way out, I met

Stephen and Ann Shine, the sort of Galwegians who make you glad you live in this city. Just that rarity: lovely, warm spirit.

In town, I bought some parchment, the real deal, and the quill pen to seal the deal. Thought about getting red wax as the seal for the document but, hey,

"Don't be showy."

Pa rang to say Keefer had collected the falcon and would collect me on Friday.

Instructed that

I was to be sure to bring supplies.

I thought,

"Oh, how I love to be *instructed*."

Especially by some half-arsed hippie drug casualty.

And then I said, unreasonably,

"Fucking nerve of him to take my falcon."

My mind responded.

"Not your bird,"

I think.

I sat down, opened a bottle of Jay, thought about Jericho.

Emerald, my former nemesis, had been a ruthless psychopath but something,

Some weird, bizarre, fucked-up mind thing, still lingered in that

I liked her.

A lot.

Now Jericho was just a poor man's Emerald. She never shone.

I had recently read *New Yorker* profiles of famous people:

Writers

Movie folk

Celebrities

By John Lahr.

The piece on Roseanne Barr described Jericho perfectly:

. . . her face and her presence have no luster.

Without makeup her definition is muted and vague, her face has little mobility.

Despite her intelligence and authority, there is something cadaverous about Roseanne,

A deadness that only rage and combat can banish.

Combat seems to make her more alive.

Something has been murdered in her; this is palpable in

The flatness of her voice, the slouch of her body,

The quicksilver shifts of mood from bombast to gloom,

The timidity and detachment behind her eyes.

She has none of the charm of Gretchen by Chelsea Cain,

Or the appeal of Lisbeth in the *Dragon Tattoo* novels.

Jericho is a dead thing.

And, soon, she'd be dead in a way that would spark in the utter darkness from whence she came.

By Christ, I swore on that.

Then I rolled out the parchment, wrote to Jericho.

Finished, I propped it against the skull she'd left for me.

I took a small envelope, put *Deoch an Doras* inside that, then opened my fridge, propped it against a bottle of Galway Hooker beer, closed the fridge gently, thought,

My *parting gift* deserves to be chilled/chilling;

On ice, as it were.

Samuel Spade's jaw was long . . .
His yellow-grey eyes were horizontal.
A hooked nose . . .
His pale brown hair grew
From high flat temples to a
Point on his forehead.
He looked rather pleasantly
Like a blond satan.
        Dashiell Hammett, *The Maltese Falcon*

I was waiting outside my apartment, a battered holdall, a crate of hooch by my Docs, the wax coat cutting the strong, bitter wind off the bay.

I missed my all-weather coat, the Garda one.

Gone with my nun.

A vintage Land Rover pulled up, the driver got out, followed by a German shepherd; the man and dog had the same vibe:

. . . *don't fuck with me.*

We'd take that under advisement.

The man said,

"Taylor!"

I nodded, he held out a large callused hand, covered in scars and recent bites, the falcon I figured. He said,

"Keefer."

He was a cross between Robert Shaw, as he was in *Jaws*, and Keith Richards, after he fell out of that tree.

Wore a Willie Nelson bandanna, biker boots over combat trousers.

He had plenty of gray-white hair, a face so lined you could see craters in it, eyes behind aviator shades, and a lean muscled body, none of it going to fat.

He growled,

"What's in the crate?"

I said,

KEN BRUEN

"A selection of Jameson, bourbon, scotch, and Bushmills.
The Bush in case you are a black Protestant."
He nearly smiled, said,
"Let's get you stored away, dude."
We did.
His voice, I would learn, was a blend of
Hipster (the sixties type)
Scottish
Surfer
Biker.
If he'd been literary, he could have played Hemingway or
James Crumley.
I sat in the shotgun seat. He put the jeep in gear and eased
into traffic, hit the music band, and the Stones'
"Sweet Virginia"
Flowed.
He asked,
"You speak American?"
I sure did, said,
"Like a good ole boy."
He went down-home South Carolina, drawled,
"I sure done check you out, boy."
That might get a little bit irritating, but I asked,
"What did you find?"
He reached into the glove department, drew out a spliff, asked,
"Do us the honor."

I did, took a hit, and passed it to him, trying to ignore the gun butt I'd spotted in the glove compartment. He drew deep, said,

"You read like a mean son of a bitch."

The dog leaned from the backseat, nuzzled my ear. Keefer said,

"You just done passed the crucial test."

I knew he meant if the dog didn't like me, my arse was gone.

The joint seemed to ease the grim line of his jaw and he expertly navigated the son of a bitch roundabout on the Headford road. He said,

"Here's the deal."

Looked at me.

I said,

"I cannot bear the excitement."

He snarled,

"I just added a new rule to the series."

A line of spittle on his mouth as he warned,

"Don't be goddamn snarky. I hate that shit, and Jagger was always running that gig."

A low rumbling from the dog.

Keefer pulled into a lay-by, said,

"I need a piss."

He and the dog disappeared into some brush.

Was it some sort of bizarre test?

It crossed my mind to fuck the hell off. He'd left the key in the ignition and, just as I thought I'd do that, a new track flowed from the speaker,

"Strange Boat"

By

The Waterboys.

The name of the foundation that began and maintained the Circle of Life Garden was Strange Boat, in honor of a young man who worked as a sound tech for the Waterboys.

Ah, the Waterboys, like the Saw Doctors, one of the great bands to come out of Galway in the eighties.

The lead singer / lyricist, Mike Scott, looked like what a rock singer should look like. Many of us believed they should have been the band that emerged globally, not U2.

If you come to Galway, get thee to the Roisin Dubh and maybe catch Mike doing the awesome "Fisherman's Blues"— almost like "Waltzing Matilda" on ludes.

(Note to millennials, if you can spare a moment from the goddamn phone: ludes were quaaludes, the chill-out drug of choice for mellow times.)

Keefer and the dog were back, got in, he burned rubber out of there. He handed me a flask, said,

"Chill, bro."

I took a slug. Wow, hard-core. Near spluttered, asked,

"The fuck's that?"

He cackled, said,

"Maker's Mark with sipping sour mash."

I drew a breath, my eyes watering, choked,

"The rules?"

He growled them

Like this:

1. Don't ask for Rolling Stones anecdotes.
2. Ten hours in the field.
3. Stay away from the armory.
4. Keefer's word is *the word*.

I lit a Red, blew out a near perfect ring that the dog tried to snatch, and said,

"I don't do rules."

He laughed, loud and lethal, the dog gave me a quick nuzzle. I asked,

"What's his name?"

You could see his face soften when the dog was the topic. He said,

"Jones."

Dilemma, was this a Stones anecdote?

Fuckit.

I asked,

"For Brian Jones?"

He sneered,

"That loser. No, I had me a heroin jones, real bad, and just as I went biblically cold turkey the dog found me, in the woods, the barrel of my gun in my mouth."

We rounded the bend where you come to Cong, bypassed the lake, pulled up on the edge of the woods. He said,

"Home."

A log cabin, frontier style, sat back in a clearing, smoke rising from a chimney, piles of neatly cut wood stacked on the side, a corral with two horses, then to the back, a small cottage, neatly white and solid. He said,

"The cottage is yours."

We put away the supplies. No sign of the falcon. I asked,

"The bird?"

He strode across wood floors, his boots resounding, opened a room to the back. There on its perch, hooded, was my falcon, looking way better than my last sighting. He said,

"This is a full-fledged falcon. She'd been trained and by an expert. Somebody should be missing a bird as valuable as this but, then, maybe the owner was shot too. I made some inquiries but no one is reporting a missing falcon."

He paused, considered, then,

"She's ready to hunt."

I gazed at her. She was fierce and beautiful, utterly still, a wonder of the sky. I involuntarily loud swallowed. Keefer said,

"She has that effect on me every time. Your buddy said you called her Maeve."

I nodded, my throat constricted. He asked,

"That your wife's name?"

I managed,

"A nun."

He did a double take, then said,

"Of course."

* * *

I checked his bookshelf, a laden one, tomes spilling out all over the shelves.

I pulled out Charles Maturin's novel *Melmoth the Wanderer*.

Published in 1820 by the Dublin vicar, it is a Faustian story.

Melmoth is the classic loner, trailing the prospect of ferocious evil in his wake.

Its most notable fan was Baudelaire.

There were other dark books:

Aleister Crowley, Kenneth Anger and his *Hollywood Babylon*,

Various bios of the Stones and Led Zep, in particular, Jimmy Page and the years of the occult.

Then Harry Crews, Hunter S. Thompson, Capote's *Music for Chameleons*.

Poetry,

The doomed ones mainly:

Anne Sexton

Ted Hughes

Robert Lowell

If you can tell a person by his library, then what did I learn about Keefer?

I muttered,

"Keep a gun ready."

Keefer provided me with a falconer's vest; it had an abundance of pockets.

KEN BRUEN

Then a thick leather glove. He surveyed me, said,
"Let's rock."

The first afternoon we spent getting the bird to fly from Keefer to me.

Scared and exhilarated me. Took a lot of time and my arm was tired from keeping it outstretched, and it involved lots of small pieces of meat as lure.

I daren't think where they came from.

I knew, there and then, though fascinated, enthralled by the falcon, I would never be able to like setting it loose to kill birds.

The first time it landed on my arm after exhausting hours, it hit with such force I nearly fell.

God almighty, the power.

Keefer ambled over the length of field to ask

How it felt.

I was almost in a trance, staring at the bird, but managed,

"Like I was hit by a Limerick hurler."

Attempts by me to tie off the hood for the bird, using my teeth to secure the length of lead from the hood, were a pitiful failure.

Darkness began to fall, thank fuck.

Keefer said,

"Okay, let's get some brews."

No sweeter words.

Keefer made dinner, asked,

"Steaks?"

There was a table cut from what seemed literally the stump of a tree. It had been polished but still maintained a rustic vibe. The falcon had been set on her perch, hooded, in the corner.

I asked,

"That to get her used to us?"

Keefer laughed, said,

"No, to get *you* used to her."

Hmm.

Keefer was standing over a battered stove, grilling the steaks, adding onions, peppers. Smelled real good, though I worried how Maeve might react.

She was making cooing sounds that had me a little on edge. Keefer turned to me, said,

"She's happy. Worry when she's silent."

That was so reassuring.

Keefer asked,

"With the steaks, a nice Lafite, from '98, I think."

Wine.

The fuck I knew from wine.

I'd drink it from the lavatory—might even have over the years. He stared at me for a moment, then laughed, said,

"Buddy, the fuck I care about wine? Pulling your chain. Grab us a coupla longnecks from the fridge."

I did. He set the steaks in front of us, large French loaf to wipe the sauce, baked spuds oozing in butter, gravy, and beans. I had an appetite.

When was the last time I had that?

I'd hazard '98, like the Lafite.

Finished, he lit up from a soft pack of Camels, said,

"Eddie Bunker's fave cig."

If he said so.

He pointed to a cupboard above the bookshelf, said,

"Have a look in there, see what bourbon you fancy."

There was a huge range of bottles, and in the corner—right in the corner—a Walther PPK.

I might know fuck all about wine but, by Christ, I know guns.

The next few days, it was evident my heart wasn't in falconry.

I loved to see the bird fly, soar, dive, and marveled at its slick, beautiful focus.

But watching it kill . . .

Not so much.

I know, I know, the violence in my past and, worse, in my heart, but the deliberate hunting down of the birds, it turned my stomach.

And I *do* understand 'tis nature but, hey fuck, it doesn't say I have to like it.

I did get a kick out of the long days in the woods, the country, but the city called to me. Keefer nodded at me during one hunt and I knew he knew.

Odd thing, as the evenings progressed, we sat into the wee hours, drinking, doing some spliffs, trading stories.

I told him more than I think I ever told anyone,

Even about the deaths of the children, my own and others. He was appropriately silent, and when I told him about Jericho, he seemed to pay extra attention.

As dawn came, he said,

"There was a small town in Ohio plagued with crows. They became a danger to crops, the local birdlife."

He laughed, said,

"They'd gone rogue, so a falcon was brought in, cleared out the crows in a matter of days. The moral is?"

The fuck I knew from morals?

He said, very quietly,

"You set a killer to catch a killer."

Later in the day, as I sweated heavily from the falcon whamming into my arm, Keefer tossed me a T-shirt, said,

"Have a fresh shirt."

It wasn't until I was falling into bed that I actually noticed the message on the T.

It read,

> *God sends your ex back into your life to*
> *See if you're still stupid.*

"Grief
    Is
        the
            Thing
                with
                    Feathers"
                    Max Porter

Meanwhile, back in Galway,
How Jericho *really* got her name.

At the Burning Man festival, where Emerald and Jericho met and hooked up, they spent most of the time on peyote and a guy had a large screen showing the gruesome, violent movie *Criminal*.

It starred Ryan Reynolds as an agent who is shot in the head and his memories are transferred to a vicious killer played by Kevin Costner.

Yeah, family fun.

Emerald had a serious hotness for Costner and, in a moment of drug euphoria, exclaimed,

"If I die, my mind will be transferred to you."

Hard-core peyote, so little wonder Jericho bought into the craziness, and when Emerald baptized her with the best tequila, chanting,

"From henceforth, thou art Jericho,"

It became so.

Jericho liked to fuck with people and tell them her name came from U2 or whatever weird shite came into her head.

She had watched *Criminal* while doing lines of coke and wondered,

"Where the hell was Alice?"

Her mobile was dead.

Jericho paced, needed action, and, of course, her primary present target was Jack Taylor. Time to go fuck with his place.

Jericho approached the door of Taylor's apartment with extreme caution.

She knew he knew she broke into his place regularly,

So would he have the brains to set a booby trap?

He wasn't in there; no one had seen him for a week.

Was he dead?

"Fuck no,"

She muttered.

She wanted/needed the joy of killing him her own self.

She set her tools on the lock.

Click.

Okay.

She opened the door slowly, her heart in ribbons. She'd seen an episode of *Fargo*, the shotgun rigged to the door, cursed,

"Where the hell is Alice?"

Girl had gone on a tear, no sign of the cow for days.

She stood in the middle of the room. On the coffee table was an envelope with

"Jericho"

In bold red marker, leaning against the skull she'd left on one of her forays.

Nervous, she picked it up, opened it oh, so carefully,
Read,

> *Sorry to miss you.*
> *Your call is important to us.*
> *I'm unavailable for a few weeks*
> *But I will be back to chat about your massacre of my friend.*
> *Meanwhile, I left a small token/trophy of our dance so far.*
> *It's on ice.*
> *That's the fridge, you dumb bitch.*
> *xxxxxx*
> *JT*

She turned, looked at the small fridge. It seemed harmless but her stomach was in knots. Would he have rigged it to explode on being opened?

She slapped herself, said,

"Get with the program. He isn't that smart."

All the same, she hesitated.

Then, steeling herself, opened the small door, realized she'd shut her eyes, cried,

"Fuck, girl, focus."

The fridge was empty save for a small red envelope propped against a bottle of Galway Hooker beer. She sneered,

"Cute, Taylor."

Took the envelope out, shook it, heard a faint rustling, then slit the flap with her long nail and out onto the coffee table fell . . .

A gold chain

With the initials *GG*, blood still encrusted on the letters.

The sound she made would have made a banshee shudder, a primeval howl of utter agony.

"Someone roll the credits on
Twenty years of love turned dark and raw
Not a technicolor love film.
(It's a brutal document—it's film noir.)
It's all played out on a borderline
And the actors are tragically
Miscast."

Tom Russell, "Touch of Evil"

Horses.

I was leaning on the corral fence, admiring the gorgeous animals.

A chestnut mare and a black stallion—they seemed perfect, like what you'd find on a box of Milk Tray. Keefer came up from the left, Jones as always loping beside him.

He was dressed in a denim jacket, torn not for fashion but from actual age, black combat pants and the dusty motorcycle boots, a black T with the near illegible *Exile on Main Street*. He looked like a Hell's Angel, if those dudes ever smiled, said,

"They're not mine."

I laughed, asked,

"What, you're a rustler too?"

His smile vanished and Jones tensed, alert to his owner's every mood. Keefer said,

"They belong to a friend. His other ones have been stolen."

I was a little skeptical, asked,

"Rustlers?"

A touch more sneer than intended leaked over the question. He gave me a look that was not aggressive but in the vicinity, said,

"A gang from the North, they steal to order . . ."

Paused, spat in the dirt, added,

"Those two are on their list."

I asked,

"Are they a worry, I mean, like dangerous?"

He lit a Camel, unfiltered, didn't offer one, showing he was angry, said,

"If beating one of the owner's crew half to death with pickaxes qualifies, I dunno, what in the *city*"—the word dripping with contempt—"you class as dangerous but, out here, we think that qualifies."

Jones had fixed me with an intense stare, the one that said,
I kind of liked you, but now . . .

We had breakfast in silence; fry-up:

Sausages

Double eggs (over easy, said Keefer)

Soda bread

Beans

And a gallon of coffee.

If we drank out of tin cups, we'd have been the complete Clint Eastwood western, bar us wearing Colts on our hips.

I said,

"I didn't mean to offend you."

Apologizing is not natural to me and I stumbled over the words. Keefer was very quiet, feeding bits of bacon to Jones who, for a German shepherd, took the food as gently as if he were in a James Herriot book. Keefer's gaze was focused on the large front window, opening out to the woods. He finally said,

"She's buried out there."

That will kill a breakfast cold.

It did.

The *she* was his wife.

He said no more about it.

That night, instead of us drinking and chatting until the small hours, he said he was tired, the bad vibe lingering. I went to my own cabin, read,

Keith Nixon

Ger Brennan

Hilary Davidson

Late, I finished off a Jay, turned in.

I think I was dreaming of my dead daughter when I was wrenched from sleep by two loud bangs. I knew the sound.

Shotgun.

I grabbed my hurley and, in just a T, underpants, and socks, ran outside.

Keefer was down, Jones on his side beside him, two men kicking the bejaysus out of Keefer, a third pulling the stallion into a horse trailer.

Without a word I was on the first guy, walloped him on the head. The other turned and, using the long swing, I took his knees out. The guy at the trailer let the horse go, reached for a hatchet, came at me, swearing,

"Where the fuck did you come out of?"

He swung the hatchet, which I sidestepped. I moved in low, smashed his face with the hurley, then stood back, adrenaline deafening me. The three were moaning, crying but not getting up, so I moved to Keefer, helped him stand. His face was bloody, one of his arms useless, but he was conscious, muttered,

"Check on the dog."

The dog was dead.

The shotgun had near obliterated his head.

I threw the shotgun as far as I could into the woods, having ejected the cartridges.

I got Keefer inside, did some makeshift first aid, gave him some painkillers and a large glass of brandy. I heard a jeep start up, ran outside to see the men take off without the horses.

I buried Jones, then went back inside, got Keefer into bed.

I checked on the falcon, and then went back outside to round up the horses.

Stopped to grab a breath at the place where Keefer had lain, said,

"The countryside is losing its appeal."

Keefer wasn't doing so well. I said,

"We need to get you to a hospital."

He shook his head, pointed to his journal, made of well-worn leather, the Stones' logo on the front, said,

"On the back page there's a number. Call, tell him I'm hurt."

I called the number, waited, then it was answered, heard a guarded,

"Yeah?"

I said,

"Keefer is hurt."

"Twenty minutes."

Click.

Okay. Fuckit, I could do curt.

Sure as shooting, a van showed up on the twenty. A man in his fifties, dressed in a beaten wax coat, not Barbour, flat cap, Wellingtons.

He walked towards me.

I said,

"He's inside."

He threw me a look of contempt, as if I thought he thought the man could be anywhere else. He was carrying a black case, went in.

I followed.

He examined Keefer, snapped at me,

"Get a bowl of hot water, clean towels."

Paused, looked around, amended,

"As clean as possible"

Two hours later, he emerged from the room, his hands swathed in blood.

I pointed to the bathroom, he went in, and—what?—he was whistling.

Emerged, ready to roll, handed me a bottle of pills, said,

"He had a serious cut across his eye, so leave the eye patch there for a day or two. I've made a splint to support his busted leg. Try to dissuade him from walking."

He paused, concerned, then,

"The knife wounds, they are a worry."

What?

I asked,

"Knife wounds?"

He looked at me like I was an ejit, said,

"I counted seven wounds. Where the hell were you when they were knifing your mate?"

I was well tired of this prick and his condescension. I said,

"Hurling."

His head snapped round, reevaluating me, then,

"Is that even a sport?"

I could play, said,

"Depends which county you support."

I looked at the pills, said,

"Jeez, these seem very big."

He sighed, said,

"Of course. They're horse tranquilizers."

Took me a minute, then the penny dropped. I said,

"You're a veterinarian."

He pulled on his wax coat, sneered,

"Well detected, Sherlock."

* * *

The next few days I tended to Keefer, changed the dressings, fed him, slowly at first; my specialty:

Irish stew

Real gravy

Carrots

Shitload of good veg

Spuds

And a wee taste of Jameson.

He was able to move to the couch in the front room, give me pointers on the falcon. I was getting better, the falcon finally responding to me and, no shit, but I felt a glow of achievement.

To see it soar, so high it was nigh invisible, then shaping itself like a missile, it dived at 200 mph to hit prey. I was chilled and filled with awe—*awe* in the biblical sense.

Keefer was recovering rapidly and I said so. He went,

"You tour with the Stones, you become bulletproof or roadkill."

He lit a spliff, drew deep, said,

"Before the awful events at Altamont, Jagger was about to launch into 'Sympathy for the Devil,'" he said.

"Strange shit happens whenever we do this song and, sure enough, all hell—Hell's Angel–style—ensued."

I said nothing. What was there to say?

He continued,

"The other day, first time in over twenty years, I played that cursed song."

I laughed nervously, said,

"Come on, there's no connection."

A knock at the door.

Keefer said,

"See? I mentioned that bloody song."

I grabbed the hurley, opened the door.

Now, of all the specters I might have anticipated, I never foresaw a

"Priest."

Keefer roared,

"Jeez, how bad am I, you sent for the priest?"

Malachy,

Who breezed past me, stared at Keefer, demanded,

"Who are you?"

Keefer sat up, laughed, said,

"I think you have that assways, Padre. Who the *fuck* are *you*?"

Christ, the whole scene was so insane I wanted to laugh. I said,

"This is Father Malachy, bishop-elect of Galway."

Malachy turned when he heard a sound from the falcon. He sneered,

"A bloody parrot. Who has a parrot?"

Keefer managed to stand, using my hurley as a crutch. I asked Malachy,

"How'd you find me?"

He looked at me with disdain, said,

"No one can hide from the Church."

Keefer said,

"And no one can hide people better."

Malachy sized up Keefer, summarized,

"I don't much like your tone, laddie."

Then he turned to me, snapped,

"Where's your manners? Don't you offer a guest a drink?"

Keefer said,

"Our last guests were lucky to get away alive."

This might have increased in hostility save for a poster.

On the wall was Jagger, looking ethereal in what appeared to be a floaty white blouse. He looked very young. Malachy gasped, went

"Is that the Hyde Park concert for Brian Jones?"

Keefer was astonished, nodded yes, asked,

"You were there?"

Malachy, lost in happy recall, mumbled,

"Oh, yeah."

I butted in,

"But you're a priest—were/are."

Malachy, still rapturous, said,

"I was a novice, visiting my aunt and my uncle. He was a Stones superfan."

Keefer, delighted, asked,

"After that, you still went ahead and became a priest?"

A hint of stubborn admiration leaked over his tone.

Malachy, suddenly sad, said,

"I couldn't disappoint my mam."

Fuck, that *mam* was heartwrenching, from a grown man about to be a bishop.

Malachy soon dispelled that feeling by rounding on me.

"Not all of us bitterly disappointed their mothers."

Keefer got a bottle of Maker's Mark, poured liberal amounts, asked,

"A toast?"

Malachy said,

"To rock 'n' roll."

They drank.

I was feeling very much the odd man out at this Stones reunion. Malachy asked,

"What is Keith really like?"

Jesus.

I thought,

Enough already.

Keefer, in mighty form, disclosed,

"A bit of a pagan."

Malachy was delighted, said,

"Sure, that's what keeps my crowd in business."

Even the falcon seemed to be cooing.

Keefer hobbled over to the bookcase, carefully slid out an album from his cherished vinyl collection, the Stones one with the cover of a pair of jeans, an actual zipper on the front—designed by Warhol.

Keefer, with reverence, intoned,

"One of the very few albums the entire band signed. Mick was tight on keeping merchandise closed down."

He handed it to Malachy like the keys to a city. Malachy, full of devilment due to the booze and an actual good time, asked,

"What would happen if I pulled that zipper down?"

He was like a child shocking his own self.

I decided to rain heavily on this fucking parade, said,

"Ye'd cover it up, as usual."

Keefer said,

"Phew, downer."

I stared at Malachy, demanded,

"Why are you here?"

His face was that of a spoiled child whose ice cream has been swiped from him. He said,

"I've a good mind not to tell you."

"Good,"

I said.

"So fuck off or out with it."

A tense silence, then Keefer said, in his *gee shucks* voice,

"Man, come on, dude, what's the gig?"

Malachy, still smarting, said,

"There's a bounty on Taylor's head."

I asked,

"How much?"

"A thousand euros."

Keefer was taken aback, said,

"That's all? Fuck, that's like . . ."

Groped for a derogatory term, found,

"Insulting."

Malachy explained,

"There's a mad bitch who first leeched off my sister, then had her killed.

"She is some sort of she-devil. I'd say she's Protestant.

"She blames Taylor for all the woes of her life so she set the bounty for word on his whereabouts."

He added,

"I'm tempted to tell her my own self now."

Before I could comment, he added,

"She has a sidekick, name of Stapleton, out on bail.

"Who imagines this? Hates Taylor, too."

Keefer lit up a spliff, said,

"Guess I'll go and collect that bounty my own self."

Malachy prepared to leave, said to me,

"You better stay in the country."

Then grudgingly added,

"I'll pray for you."

He shook Keefer's hand, said,

"'Twas a joy to meet you."

Keefer, equally delighted, said,

"I'll vote for you as bishop."

Malachy looked crestfallen, said,

"The people don't get a vote."
Keefer could have said,
"See, that's the problem right there."
But he let it slide.
After Malachy's departure, Keefer gave me the look, asked,
"How much do you think Jericho will like the country?"
I nearly smiled, said,
"Not a whole lot, I'm thinking."

The annals
Of human wisdom
Fall silent
When faced
With the feral
In us.

William Giraldi, *Hold the Dark*

Keefer's face was still in ruinous shape, which aided the mission he was on.

He was dressed in a blend of intimidation and unknowability.

Meaning, a bank manager would not turn him away, nor would a first-class hotel refuse him accommodation.

But all would be on edge, very careful in their response, because of not just his attire, his brutalized appearance, but the vibe, the one that implied,

"Do not fuck with me."

He wore a long duster, very battered cowboy boots, a Willie Nelson swirl of bandannas, and his hands were gnarled, mangled, like he'd wrangled steers and very recently.

To add confusion to apprehension, he spoke in a soft, dulcet tone that was in the neighborhood of sarcasm and irony.

He found Jericho without any bother, just searched for a dive where bottom-feeders fed.

It was in an alley running parallel to the old docks and, incredibly enough, had a bouncer on the door. Keefer smiled.

The guy was built and eyed Keefer carefully, went

"Haven't seen you before."

Keefer reached into his duster and the guy flinched. Keefer took out a cig, fired up, asked,

"There a smoking ban in there?"

The guy wondered if this might be some sort of health inspection sting, so said,

"'Tis against the law."

Keefer ground the cig beneath his boot, said,

"We wouldn't want to fuck with that."

Went inside.

Metallica were on full blast, the crowd in a small smoky room, one long bar and scattered tables. Keefer spotted Jericho in a corner. She was as both Malachy and Taylor had described. She looked like deep trouble.

She was engrossed in conversation with a guy.

Keefer went to the bar. The woman behind the counter, a woman who'd seen too many mornings, all of them blank, snarled,

"Yeah?"

Keefer gave her a full smile, which, with his battered face, made him look downright sinister. He said,

"Let me compliment you on the warmth of your welcome. Are you by any chance related to the charmer on the door?"

Now she actually hissed, went

"He's my husband."

Keefer rocked back on his heels, said,

"A keeper. Now, what do you suggest?"

As he eyed the beer selection, which seemed to be Bud and, surprise, Bud, she suggested,

"Get your ugly face to somewhere else."

He leaned over, pinched her cheek before she could move, said,

"You minx, let's be having a Bud."

In shock, she automatically gave him the brew. He said,

"I'll be back."

Strolled over to Jericho. Stapleton eyed him with undisguised malice.

Keefer stood a foot from them, gauging the vibe.

Stapleton he dismissed as a bigmouthed petty thief cliché, but Jericho . . . now here was swirling dark energy, a girl destined for destruction. She had a pretty face but decay of the soul threw a shadow over her.

Keefer grabbed a stool and in one fluid motion sat. Stapleton immediately spat,

"Bad idea, asshole."

Keefer never looked at him, locked eyes with Jericho, and, as Stapleton reached to his jeans, lashed out, grabbed his arm in a crushing grip, said very quietly,

"I wasn't talking to you. Now, that excuse of a knife you have, do *not* reach for it or I'll make you eat it."

Jericho was amused; she lived for chaos, asked,

"Who might you be?"

Keefer said,

"The guy who knows where to find Jack Taylor."

There was a beat as Jericho assessed Keefer, then,

"He do that to you?"

Keefer nodded, waited.

Stapleton asked,

"So where is he?"

Keefer reached into his coat, took out a piece of paper, said,

"This is the location of where he goes on a Thursday, same time, same place."

Jericho was suspicious, asked,

"Why?"

Keefer let out a lengthy sigh as if it pained him to tell, then,

"He is training some kind of bird. It's the only time he is full preoccupied. If you want to take him by surprise, then that's the time, the place."

The mention of the bird gave Jericho a slight shudder but she shrugged it off.

Jericho reached for the paper. Keefer smiled, said,

"Uh-oh, the small matter of a thousand euros."

Jericho looked at Stapleton, said,

"Give him four hundred."

Stapleton didn't move.

Keefer stood up, said,

"See yah."

Jericho tried,

"Half now, half when we, um, see him."

Keefer shook his head.

Stapleton snapped,

"How do we know you're not some bullshit artist?"

Keefer didn't answer, just held Jericho's stare. She blinked first, said,

"Okay, but you drive us there, that's the deal."

Exactly what Keefer hoped but he stood as if weighing his options, then,

"Be here tomorrow, two sharp, and have the money."

Meanwhile, back at the ranch, so to speak.

I practiced for hours every day with the falcon and a scarecrow.

I'd stand at the edge of the field, having covered the scarecrow with chunks of meat, and then release the falcon.

Took a while but, finally, I barely had the hood off the bird when it flew high, turned, and zoomed on the scarecrow.

Filled with a grim satisfaction, I said,

"Good bird."

And you will never
Know the depth of your heart
Until you are presented with
The opportunity for revenge.
Only then will you know
What you are capable of.

Cormac McCarthy, *The Counselor*

The
Day
of
the
Falcon

The law relating to falconry:

> *The falconer must have knowledge of*
> And
> Comply with
> *The legislation concerning quarry.*
> *In simple terms,*
> *The species which a falcon can be flown at*
> *Are divided into three groups:*
> *1. Game*
> *2. Species not under wildlife protection*
> *3. Vermin*
> > I paid special attention to the meaning of *vermin*.

Keefer picked up the deadly duo at two o'clock as arranged.
He said,
"The smart-ass rides in the back and you, dear, you ride shotgun."
A look passed between Stapleton and Jericho but they complied.
They drove in silence until Keefer asked Stapleton,
"You bring your knife, boy?"
Stapleton sneered, said,
"You'll see soon enough, shithead."

Keefer hit the sound system and "Street Fighting Man" filled the jeep.

Jericho was in a zone and seemed utterly focused. Stapleton fidgeted and seemed set to rumble. Keefer said,

"Try to keep it in your pants, boy."

They arrived at a country road. The time was ten to three. Keefer pointed to a field, said,

"Three on the button, Taylor enters the field."

Jericho got out, took a long blade from her tote, slipped it up her sleeve. Stapleton made to move but Keefer suddenly turned, a sawed-off magically in his hands, said,

"Sit tight, boy."

Jericho stared for a moment, then said,

"Okay, that's cool. I won't be long."

Keefer said to Stapleton,

"You have a choice. Follow her into the field . . ."

He let the weight of that settle, then,

"Or . . ."

He pointed with the gun barrel.

"You can take *the high road,* down that way, to town."

My back was turned to Jericho as she came into the field and I let her get to within a knife blade, then turned, said,

"Meet Maeve."

With my free hand, I threw a bag of meat at her face, it poured over her hair, face, and down onto her shoulders. She gasped, went

"What the fuck?"

I said,

"Not that it really counts but you'll find there are forty-eight chunks of meat, like the number of wounds on my friend."

I moved to the back of the field, said,

"Whatever you do, don't run."

Then I released the falcon.

Jericho ran.

It was silent for a moment as the falcon climbed high, then folded itself, zoomed down. I headed back toward the house, screams ringing out across an empty meadow.

Before I reached the house, I heard two blasts of the shotgun, knew Keefer had finished whatever was stirring after the falcon attack.

Keefer and I were sitting before a log fire, strong glasses of bourbon in our hands. He was wearing a faded T-shirt with the Grateful Dead logo. A faded date underneath identified it as the year of Altamont, when the Hell's Angels killed a fan in front of the Stones' stage. You'd have to know your Stones mythology to know how heavily Jerry Garcia and the Dead were involved in the logistics of the biker band being hired.

The Angels were given five hundred dollars to buy beer as the price of them providing security.

I asked,

"What about her . . ."

Paused,

"Remains?"

Keefer gave a sardonic smile, said,

"I'll bury her with the others."

A chill briefly flitted through the room, then Keefer asked,

"Want a spliff?"

I nodded and he asked,

"Music?"

I said,

"Got a version of 'Galway Girl'?"

He smiled, asked,

"Does a falcon fly?"

About the author

KEN BRUEN is one of the most prominent Irish crime writers of the last two decades. He received a doctorate in metaphysics, taught English in South Africa, and then became a crime novelist. He is the recipient of two Barry Awards, two Shamus Awards and has twice been a finalist for the Edgar Award. He lives in Galway, Ireland.